Oh Selene!

Oh Daddy!

(Playlists/Miscellanea)

Of GOEW

[Title Cards Version]

UpSet Press

PO Box 200340
Brooklyn, NY 11220

upsetpress.org

**Crystalline Green:
(Playlists/Miscellanea) Of GOEW**

UpSet Press is an independent, not-for-profit (501c3 tax exempt)
organization advancing thought-provoking works of literature, including
translated works, to promote curiosity/transformation, i.e., to upset the
status quo.

—

ISBN 978-1-937357-85-6
Library of Congress Control Number:
2022942904
Printed in US
First Edition [Title Cards Version]

—

Book and cover design by
Jessica D'Elena-Tweed

Contents

About the playlists

The original playlists in Green Of Each Window (GOEW)—Stay, All Night, If 6 Was 9, Honey Man, Distant Dream, Summertime, Beautiful, All My Lovers—were created independent of the writing of GOEW. It was only in the early stages of revising that it struck me to pair the songs from the playlists with the poems, scenes, section headings, etc. At first, the pairings were obvious and easy. But completing the task proved arduous and dizzying, and even required (admittedly) some slight revision of the original playlists.

After the songs were paired, I compiled them sequentially according to the narrative of GOEW, and then separated them by section. This revealed four new playlists: Union Hotel, The Beautiful Made Thing, Love Bomb, and Postcard from Angel Falls. Each featured the songs from the original playlists in a new sequence, establishing a new emotional arc. Furthermore, these four playlists, born incidentally from the initial act of pairing, can be combined to create one complete playlist of GOEW, since they run sequential to each other.

Then, just when I thought I was done (and relieved to be done), I felt this impulse to create new playlists from/for the interludes—the front/back matter, the bridges between poems, miscellanea—that didn't have any songs paired with them initially. (Eros) [Paris] was the first playlist born of this impulse. Then, (Counterfactuals) [Lima]; (Despair) [NYC]; (Reverie) [LA]; etc. Each follows the same formula (see p. 168). Any one of the interludes' playlists can be integrated with the complete playlist of GOEW to comprise one epic playlist, in which every text inhabits an echo, or infers a listening space off the page. Moreover, the interludes' playlists can be substituted to subtly affect the mood, or tenor, since they run parallel to each other. In this way, one can create multiple versions of a GOEW playlist, i.e. The Complete Playlist of GOEW – (Eros) [Paris] Version, or The Complete Playlist of GOEW – (Despair) [NYC] Version, etc.

There are 62 interludes' playlists included herein. (There is potential to go on, ad infinitum.) The chronology is murky, but I have separated out the first 31, and the latter 31, as two coronas; each comprising a section of this book. To determine the sequence of the two sections, I applied the same formula mentioned above utilizing all track 27s. I titled them "Interludes' Playlists Corona #1" & "Interludes' Playlists Corona #2." I added the qualifying subtitle, "Title Cards Version" to the book because track 27 represents the titles of the respective interludes' playlists.

Lastly, I created a complete playlist of Crystalline Green, including its interludes. There can be multiple versions of a complete Crystalline Green playlist, too. However, unlike the multiple versions of a complete GOEW playlist, which could go on forever if one were to continue creating new interludes' playlists—the maximum number of versions for a complete Crystalline Green playlist would be thirty one. One version for each track in the formula.

And here begins
the difficult task
of trying to understand
another person.

—Chris Kraus, *"ALIENS & ANOREXIA"*

opera
opera
(an opera)

(Sans Interludes)

Narrative playlists

(Sonance) Of Applause

I Want You to Want Me–Live at Nippon Budokan, Japan | Cheap Trick

Everything should be listened to
twice, at least! Once with headphones,
eyes closed, straight through.
Then, again, with a lover, or friends,
over foreplay, lovemaking,
drinks, conversation.

Listening's the closest thing to time travel,
or teleporting. It's how you know
you're not alone, in your yearning,
sadness or joy, absent any theater.
It's how you see, really see others
as versions of yourself, a little ahead of or behind you.

Everything's the same, formulaic, and not the same, fickle.
Everything, though, is poetry. That graduates to song.

Union Hotel

Temporarily Yours | Cristina

Do I Move You?	Nina Simone	2:44
The Line	Mood Rings	3:23
Stay	Zedd, Alessia Cara	3:29
No Judgement	Niall Horan	2:55
Tonight You Might	Synthia, Lady Wray	3:51
Lost and Lookin'	Sam Cooke	2:11
What's Your Pleasure?	Jessie Ware	4:37
You Know How to Make Me Feel so Good	Susan Cadogan	5:01
Beautiful	Qveen Herby	3:23
Dive In	Trey Songz	4:12
I'm The Man, That Will Find You	Connan Mockasin	5:01
Dopamine	BØRNS	3:44
Alles ist gut	PA Sports	3:56
L-O-V-E – Long Version	Joss Stone	2:48
I'm Gonna Do My Thing	Royal Deluxe	3:08
A Real Hero	College & Electric Youth	4:27
Gemini	Knox Fortune	3:02
Numb	Portishead	3:57
My Neck, My Back (Lick It)	Khia	3:42
Shape of You	Ed Sheeran	3:53
Moonlight	dhruv	2:38
PILLOWTALK	ZAYN	3:22
The Sixth Night: Waking	Muriel Rukeyser	0:24
Baby	Donnie & Joe Emerson	4:09
Disco Man	Remi Wolf	3:11
Don't Let Me Be Misunderstood	Nina Simone	2:46
Nannou [EP Version]	Aphex Twin	4:15
No Silhouette	DPR IAN	2:28
Bitter	Meshell Ndegeocello	4:15
Anda Jaleo	Paco de Lucia, Andres Batista, et al	2:25
Make It Fast, Make It Slow	Rob	5:25
All Night – Unfinished	Jai Paul	3:12
Strangelove	Depeche Mode	4:54
Under Your Spell	Desire	4:55

77	77	4:08
Cry in the Wind	Cry in the Wind	5:16
FALLING	FALLING	2:13
		2h 13m

The Beautiful Made Thing

Reverie-Above & Beyond Club Mix | **Above & Beyond, Zoë Johnston**

All About U	Rai-Elle	2:55
I Just Wanna Lay Around All Day In Bed With You	The Coup	5:15
Oh Shooter	Robin Thicke	4:36
Get on Top	Tim Buckley	6:32
Talkin' fame and music	Bob Marley & Dermot Hussey	1:51
I Shot the Sheriff	Bob Marley & The Wailers	7:12
I'm Good, I'm Gone	Lykke Li	3:08
American Money	BØRNS	4:20
Feelin' Lovely	Connan Mockasin, Devonté Hynes	3:51
Kiss U Right Now	Duckwrth	3:14
He Knows a Lot of Good Women	Love	3:15
Alive	Krewella	4:50
Motorbike	Leon Bridges	3:07
Touch Me	Victoria Monét, Kehlani	3:07
Moonage Daydream	David Bowie	4:39
Fancy Man	Devendra Banhart	2:59
Licking An Orchid	Yves Tumor, James K	4:37
Beautiful Escape	Tom Misch, Zak Abel	4:36
Love U Better	Victoria Monét	3:51
We Should Be Together	Pia Mia	3:43
Disco Tits	Tove Lo	3:43
Fuckboy	BAUM	3:00
I'll Be There For You/You're All I Need	Method Man, Mary J. Blige	3:40
Feels Like Summer	Childish Gambino	4:56
Something Just Like This	The Chainsmokers, Coldplay	4:06
Jaguar	Victoria Monét	3:30
Huit octobre 1971	Cortex	4:26
Tell Me	Neil Frances, The Undercover Dream Lovers	3:17
You	Yellow Days	4:05
I Want You	Erykah Badu	10:52
Pony	Ginuwine	4:11
The Piano Has Been Drinking (Not Me)	Tom Waits	3:40

You Know I'm No Good	Amy Winehouse	4:16
Soul Control	Jessie Ware	3:59
One And Four (AKA Mr. Day)	John Coltrane	7:36
Birthday Suit	Kesha	2:55
Hurt	Johnny Cash	3:36
Come Over	Ce'Cile, ZJ Chrome	3:22
Mr. Sexy Man	Nellie Tiger Travis	4:09

2h 45m

Love Bomb

Blackout Days | Phantogram

Move Like This	Ric Wilson, Terrace Martin	4:04
Summertime	Louis Armstrong, Ella Fitzgerald	4:57
Heartbeats – Live	The Knife	4:21
Woman Is A Word	Empress Of	3:16
Crimewave (Crystal Castles Vs.) [David Wolf Edit]	HEALTH	2:40
500 Days of Summer	Grady	1:53
LAVENDER	Dounia	2:18
Please Don't Touch [The Golden Filter Remix]	Polly Scattergood, The Golden Filter	6:25
You Don't Love Me (No, No, No) - Extended Mix	Dawn Penn	4:37
Yannis & the Dragon	Christodoulos Halaris	6:57
Company	Tinashe	3:39
Legend In His Own Mind	Gil Scott-Heron	3:40
Pussy Is God	King Princess	3:25
Good Pussy	Alia Kadir	3:02
Serial Lover	Kehlani	2:25
Aquarius/Let The Sunshine In	The 5th Dimension	4:48
Sugar on My Tongue	Talking Heads	2:36
Masquerade	Clan of Xymox	3:54
Mysterium Tremendum	Christopher Young	1:40
Cherry-coloured Funk	Cocteau Twins	3:12
A Day	Clan of Xymox	6:40
Nights in White Satin [Single Version]	The Moody Blues	4:24
My Angel	Horace Andy	2:54
Summer 2020	Jhené Aiko	3:15
Angel of the Morning	Juice Newton	4:14
Go To Town	Doja Cat	3:37
I Wanna Roll With You	Connan Mockasin	5:44
Birthday Sex	Jeremih	3:45
The Man Who Couldn't Afford to Orgy	John Cale	4:33
Love Bomb	N.E.R.D	4:35
Hit the Back	King Princess	3:23

Eternity	Noah Collette, Sonia Tavik, Kenndoe	3:21
Pretender	Black Marble	3:22
Get You The Moon	Kina, Snøw	2:58
Lights Down Low	MAX	3:43
SUMMER	BROCKHAMPTON	3:24
Softness As A Weapon	Kindness	5:08

2h 23m

Postcard from Angel Falls

Paradise | Griff

Alright	Adonis Bosso	3:18
Love Language	Kehlani	3:32
Love Is A Drug	Empress Of	2:39
Levitating	Dua Lipa, DaBaby	3:22
I Lost Everything	Sam Cooke	3:23
End of the World	Anika	2:56
Silhouette of the Pinnacle	Riff Raff, DJ Whoo Kid	3:53
Thinking About Your Body	Josh Milan, Louie Vega	11:10
(Louie Vega Dance Ritual Mix)		
Don't Wait Up	Oh He Dead	4:10
Love You Like A Love Song	Selena Gomez & The Scene	3:08
Flower (Girly-Sound Version)	Liz Phair	2:47
O.P.P	Naughty By Nature	4:30
Stay	Rihanna, Mikky Ekko	4:00
All Night	Bree Runway	3:38
If 6 Was 9	Jimi Hendrix	5:34
Honey Man	Tim Buckley	4:11
Distant Dream	John Carpenter	3:51
Summertime	Stick Figure, Citizen Cope	3:58
Beautiful	Bazzi	2:57
All My Lovers	Black Tape For A Blue Girl	4:01
I Want Your Love	Chromatics	6:40
I'll Wait	Kygo, Sasha Alex Sloan	3:34
Coney Island Winter	Garland Jeffreys	3:47

1h 35m

(a g e s t a l t)

{Suite

for

Kill Me With Your Love | One True God

Selene}

LOVE = TEMPORARY INSANITY

(Climax) Of Arrival

There is a fifth mode, a clandestine listening space
for the highly sensitive to melt into the lyrics.
An auditorium for empathy. Abduction as role play.
Title cards in an opera. An orchestra of thunder.

But this hotel is like all hotels. You adorn it with meaning,
sketch its skyline on a postcard you save, but never send.
When you fly, you feel the departure more than the arrival.
Sex is how you heal, how you reinvent yourself.

Home is a prison cell. Dreams are your escape.
Eternity is an erection that lasts too long.
Going to the club is innocent. Gazing at the moon is more wanton.
Death is another version of sex on an intergalactic level.

When you come, you feel the arrival more.
Everything else is backstory. Or encore.

PARATAXIS

Come on Doom, Let's Party | Emily Wells

ADONIS: To go from the stage to the audience, from playing the piano, emitting music, to being someone who hears it, perceiving melody... That's what it means to be a glare.

SELENE: Choke me.

ADONIS: I want to be the one that makes you feel the deepest. Preferably, the deepest happiness! But the deepest sadness is profound too.

SELENE: Wait, go slow.

ADONIS: I'm ready to blow everything up.

SELENE: You mean blossom.

ADONIS: Yes, bloom.

SELENE: Come on me, daddy.

ADONIS: Wow!

SELENE: It feels like a lot.

ADONIS: Love?

SELENE: Falling into your sigh.

Stop-Motion Animation

In The Evening (It's So Hard To Tell Who's Going To Love You The Best) | Karen Dalton

1. Oh Selene!

The deepest exhale through the mouth.
The eyes affixed to Selene rising to pee.
The knees straightening in a supine stretch.
The folding of the cock into the inguinal canal.

2. Oh World!

The deepest inhale through the nose.
The eyes shut to beaming lights.
The knees bent in readiness to leap.
The unfolding of a man into an arrow.

MOONLIGHT DENSETSU

Moonlight Densetsu (From "Sailor Moon) | Harpsona

ADONIS: When I close my eyes, I conjure you, I taste you, then I burrow in you.

SELENE: I missed you!

ADONIS: I missed you more!

SELENE: I'm the one who retreats.

ADONIS: I'm the one who burrows.

(They walk through the park holding hands.)

SELENE: It's from dreams, premonitions, I can sometimes tell that something bad is going to happen before it does. Like, I just know.

ADONIS: Only bad things? What about good things?

SELENE: It's never been directed towards me specifically, but more like things that affect others. Good things are harder.

ADONIS: Do you warn them?

SELENE: My radar is only tuned in to the bad for some reason.

ADONIS: It's a gift. A power.

SELENE: It's not really situations where I can warn someone. It's more like after something happens, I realize I had a foreboding feeling.

ADONIS: Hm. Is the foreboding feeling connected to an individual? Or is it a broader foreboding? Like something bad is going to happen, but I'm not sure to who?

SELENE: A mix. One time it happened when my friends went out and I stayed behind. I just knew something bad was going to happen. They got into a car accident.

ADONIS: You're a mystic. Trust your feelings.

SELENE: What do they say about me?

ADONIS: That you're attuned to feelings, above or outside articulation. They help you in your decisions. There are certain truths that need to be felt, not explained. Or, can't be explained. But the feelings communicate or resonate somehow in other ways. I'd say you have that intuition. It was Maya Angelou who said you don't remember what people say to you, but you remember how they make you feel. Poets and mystics are similar. As poets we obsess with articulating feelings. Mystics have other tools, ways.

SELENE: Ye.

ADONIS: I have my poems and playlists. You have your tarot cards and premonitions.

SELENE: I like hearing you talk.

ADONIS: I like talking to you.

SELENE: I'm glad.

(Adonis gives Selene his heart, by way of the moon, and another one regenerates in its place, bigger, better, more capable of love. Selene eats his heart, by way of snow falling, and this nourishes her, warms her, excites her.)

Warm Dream, Ocean Groove

Sex Sounds | Lil Tjay

Freshly showered and
smelling like a warm dream, I
enter the ocean

that is Selene's eyes.
When she takes my cock in her
mouth, she looks at me

looking at her. My
cock swells, stiffens, slides into,
out of, her mouth. I

caress her temples.
She runs her hands over my
waist, thighs, ass, nipples.

I climb off of her,
"I like making you hard," she
says. I climb back on

top of her, spread her
legs, enter her. "I melted
from look in your eyes."

"How was I looking
at you?" she teases. "Like you
were seeing me with

aplomb!
That's it! (Moaning) You looked so
confident

taking my cock in
your mouth. It made me melt and
get hard at same time.

My entire body
fissured!" (Convulsing) "I want
you to cum inside

me. Don't stop!" (Pounding)

TULIPS (OR BLOOM)

fever dream | **mxmtoon**

ADONIS: (Flowers) For you.

SELENE: Thank you! You make me feel whole, and grounded, and seen.

ADONIS: You make me feel young, and meaningful, and sexy.

SELENE: I can't stop thinking of us doing unspeakable things in your office.

ADONIS: You're going to get me fired.

SELENE: I don't want to get you fired, but I do want to excite you!

ADONIS: I want it, too. I want you crazy and pornographic. I want you sane and sharing secrets with me. I want both! All of it!

SELENE: If anything, your coworkers will be jealous of your amazing sex life with your amazing girlfriend.

ADONIS: I feel so blessed to have you. I pinch myself every day.

SELENE: I feel the same.

(They go into Adonis' office.)

ADONIS: (Locking door) Everything good in my life has come from three rules. One, say yes more than no.

SELENE: I do that already.

ADONIS: Two, choose action over inaction. If you're debating going to a party or not, go to the party.

SELENE: Ye.

ADONIS: It'll lead to some regrets. But it's better to regret doing things than not doing things. (Nuzzles her)

SELENE: I agree. (Retreats)

ADONIS: Three, shed your ego.

SELENE: That's hard!

ADONIS: That's how you'll truly see others.

SELENE: What if you shed your ego, but you still lust for others? Then, will you see them? (Opens her blouse) Truly?

Hymn for Selene

She's a Rainbow | The Rolling Stones

Once upon a time
there was a beautiful, young woman...
Her name was Selene.

She had a quiet courage.
She was thoughtful in her daring,
and other matters.

She had a yearning, a deep yearning
for community, for love,
for art, film, music,

what made life more pleasant,
more enjoyable, for curating
life's blissful moments.

She curated time the way a painter
mixes colors, the way a DJ
mixes songs, the way a pastry chef

mixes ingredients.
She could stretch it out
to linger in intervals of lovemaking,

or she could hasten it
to diminish time away from a lover.
She could look up at the sky

and name all the constellations.
She could look into your eyes
and discern all your intentions,

the depth, the integrity of each one.
She whispered with animals and shadows,
and they circled her like bodyguards,

sniffing, screening out strangers who approached her.
And even though she was conscious of her magnificence,
she still had a modesty, an uncertainty, to her.

She still had an open-mindedness,
a willingness to listen, to question,
to perceive new modes of thinking, and seeing.

She was a fairy who became a mystic
who became the moon
who became a woman.

This is her origin myth.
This is her (eternal) flight.

THE DIAL

Bizarre Love Triangle | **New Order**

DEVIL: Thank you for this interview.

SELENE: You're welcome.

DEVIL: How would you describe *Green Of Each Window*?

SELENE: From the perspective of Adonis, a man cheats on his wife, feels guilt, but at the same time feels a deep yearning for new life, new love, new meaning. He loses himself, or exhausts himself in this pursuit, and ultimately succumbs to his exhaustion. In a sense, from the start, he was a fatalist, and derived meaning from orchestrating impossible or unsustainable relationships.

DEVIL: I wasn't expecting that.

SELENE: I'm not done. From the perspective of Thaïs, a woman wants a divorce, partly because she feels fettered and unfulfilled, and partly because she feels new love for a new man, and would like a do-over at marriage, at life. She has a deep yearning for more poetry in her life, and more romance. She adores being the subject of Adonis' poems, and so, she throws herself at him. She wears her immodesty as lingerie. Unexpectedly, sadly, she is stricken with cancer before she can cultivate a new life. She is robbed of her do-over.

DEVIL: Harsh.

SELENE: From the perspective of Nico, a young woman seeks adventure, and experience, as source material for making art, inhabiting Eros, and feeling sexy. She yearns to live a double life, where she can break down stereotypes, and explore taboos anonymously. She is turned on by having a secret identity. She dresses up to play a part, the lead part, in a film she wishes to one day make. She quickly discovers, in dressing up, that the part takes over, and she becomes the part, she prefers the part.

DEVIL: Fascinating.

SELENE: Overall though, it's about lust. A deluge of yearning.

DEVIL: The illogic of love.

SELENE: Its implosion!

DEVIL: Touché! What about you? Are you the transcendental muse?

SELENE: I'm a cheetah, an endangered species. **(Sigh)** Adonis, Nico, Thaïs, they're all muses to each other. Except for me, they're not muses. They're cautionary tales. I'm living my best hoe life.

DEVIL: By chance, are you on Tinder?

SELENE: No. But I'm on Sugar Baby.

DEVIL: Oh.

SELENE: What paper are you from again?

DEVIL: The Dial.

SELENE: Oh.

Orlandos of the Sea

Exist for Love | AURORA

Some nights I sense you drifting away
like the tide going out
on these nights I cling to you a little tighter
because I'm willing to drown for you

but my intention isn't to drown
my intention is to teach you how to swim
in the ocean it's much easier
you can just float with the currents (don't fight them)

like two koi fish swimming circles
the radius of our bodies
being carried away by a world
that goes on without noticing us

the yin and yang of hotel trysts
gazing at the moon or the film *Orlando*

Warm Dream/Hymn Mashup

Moanin' | Charles Mingus

There is a curiosity
that underlies her grace.

She doesn't so much yearn
for the sublime as she inhabits it!

She speaks opera.
Her language is song.

Her song is instrumental,
more guttural than literal.

Lyrics are too contrived
to capture her essence.

She is a buddha
in a cheerleader's body.

Her body is more mist
(steam from a hot shower) than flesh.

Her smell is more cosmos than garden.
Her eyes are more mirrors than windows.

Her torso is an acoustic guitar.
her belly a mezzo-soprano

crying out, "Fuck! Yes!
I'm coming!"

SELENE'S JOINT

Heavenly | Cigarettes After Sex

(Bustling restaurant)

ADONIS: You did it.

SELENE: Ye. My own weed restaurant.

ADONIS: Amazing.

SELENE: Will you stay for dinner?

ADOIS: Of course.

SELENE: I have a private room for us in the back.

ADONIS: Excellent.

SELENE: Have you seen the menu? Every dish has weed in it.

ADONIS: What if I pass out?

SELENE: I'll resuscitate you.

ADONIS: You keep saving me.

SELENE: You keep testing me.

ADONIS: It's you I want to bury me.

SELENE: I don't want to bury you. I rather fuck you.

ADONIS: Me too! But your memory...

SELENE: What about it?

ADONIS: (Reluctantly) You don't remember...

SELENE: It's not memory. You're part of me now. You're inside me.

ADONIS: I'm here because of you.

SELENE: You didn't die. Not in my arms.

ADONIS: I want to stay inside you forever.

SELENE: Your cock in my mouth?

ADONIS: Yes.

SELENE: Your tongue in my ass?

ADONIS: Yes.

SELENE: Your big cock in my small pussy?

ADONIS: Yes, yes...

SELENE: Deeper, deeper...

ADONIS: So deep I die...

SELENE: (Moaning) Don't stop. (Grunting) Don't you fucking stop... (Reviving Adonis) You see, my love. Not death. Heaven.

Dear Selene,

Daddy | Ramsey

You are my swan song,
and the love of my life.

When I die, I want you at my funeral.
If you can, if you even hear about it.

Here is Devil's phone number, _____
in case I ghost you,

because I would never ghost you.
I want you to wear your black dress,

sheer top, fishnet stockings (your MCR outfit).
I want you to look at all the pictures of me.

Then I want you to take from your pocketbook
that picture of you and me, from Ocean Grove,

that you put in the white frame,
and had up in your room—

       (Did you put it up each time I came over,
       or leave it up? Inconsequential now!)—

place it on a table
among all the other pictures,

scan the room for marigold,
and walk out of there free,

the goddess (and witch) you always were,
and start over with a sense you already won.

You'll still be young and beautiful,
and I'll be with you, inside you always.

And just one last time, look up at the moon,
and call me *Daddy*.

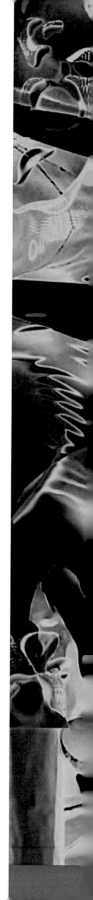

Crème de la Crème

Caramel | Connan Mockasin

Of all the sweets
in this pastry shop—the passion

fruit tart, the powdered
chocolate croissant, the heavenly

cinnamon roll (your favorite)—
the sweetest of all

is you, when I burrow
in you, and then

you swallow me, and then
I beckon you for that

       smudged kiss.

flight

(A   TO)

INTERLUDES'

PLAYLISTS

Infinity | Jaymes Young

CORONA #1

GOEW Mise en Scène

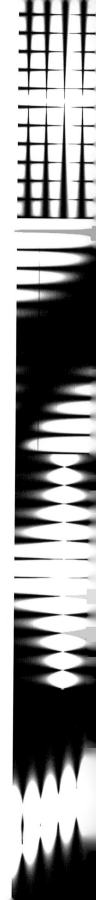

From You Animal Machine | Eleni Sikelianos, Roger Green

There are four view modes:
frontal, mirror, peripheral, counterfactual.
Then, there's a photograph of looking.
On the back of the photo: date and time. Could be any place.
A person's looking at the world
while listening to music. Could be anyone.
But it's you. This life.
Could be a cemetery. That too is an audience.
The music's inferred by performance.
You join the performance,
begin to dance
in a nuanced way, become a star.
A shooting star, a dying star.
Such is performance.
There's an encore,
an afterparty.
Everyone's bride and groom,
lock and key.
There's the specter of arrest.
This is the literature of the future.
Everything's propaganda,
for mature audiences.
The night sky
points to no return.
Everyone has PTSD.
There's so much to clean up or hide
before you can relax.
There's a curtain call,
a standing ovation,
the flash of cameras, a roving spotlight.
You see yourself in the audience
as if looking back in time. To a more innocent time.

(Despair) [New York City]

Stuck on Repeat	Little Boots	3:21
Sexy sexy man	King Barry C Thomas	3:22
Forever Young - Fast Version	Bob Dylan	2:48
Empire State Of Mind	JAY-Z, Alicia Keys	4:36
Strangers	Portishead	3:57
The End of the World	Sharon Van Etten	2:58
Requiem For A Tower	London Music Works	4:10
I Found The F	Broadcast	2:21
WALKTHROUGH	Myles Yachts, BOS	2:54
El Reloj	Los Pasteles Verdes	3:29
Stepping Razor	Peter Tosh	5:47
Pull Up To The Bumper	Grace Jones	4:41
Here Come De Honey Man	Herbie Hancock	3:58
Beat It	Michael Jackson	4:18
Love Lies	Khalid, Normani	3:21
King	Niykee Heaton	5:22
Loaded Gun	6LACK	3:18
Surrender	Suicide	3:48
Summer Madness	Kool & The Gang	4:17
Feel The Way I Want	Caroline Rose	4:03
Moody!	Jean Deaux, Saba	1:45
Treat Me Like Fire	LION BABE	4:10
New Sensations (Valerie Solanas Was Right)	Vixen	5:27
Talk To Strangers	Saul Williams	2:39
Love's a Loaded Gun	Alice Cooper	4:11
Cleopatron (Drunk on Me)	Diamond White	3:09
New York City	Lenny Kravitz	6:22
Love Come Down	Blond Ambition	4:02
I Close My Eyes	Clan of Xymox	6:54
Kiss Of Fire	Louis Armstrong	3:06
Poverty Train	Laura Nyro	4:15

2h 3m

(Stars) [Lay You Down]

All Rivers at Once	Sevdaliza	4:45
Sextape	Deftones	4:01
Stargirl Interlude	The Weeknd, Lana Del Rey	1:51
Spill The Milk	Eartheater	3:39
Navy Light	Labyrinth Ear	3:07
New To You	Calvin Harris, Normani, Tinashe, Offset	5:02
Why She Is Hiding in the Other Man's Eyes	IIIIIIIIIIIIIIIIIIII	5:04
U Already Know	112	3:18
Champagne Coast	Blood Orange	4:52
Just For Us Pt. 2	benny blanco	1:55
Get You	Daniel Caesar, Kali Uchis	4:38
Falling	DRAMA	3:32
Moment Musical	Krzysztof Komeda	2:09
The Sweetest Taboo	Sade	4:37
Cellophane	FKA twigs	3:24
Belong to You	Sabrina Claudio, 6LACK	3:05
Repetition	Purity Ring	3:38
Chemtrails Over The Country Club	Lana Del Rey	4:31
Strip Tease	Alain Goraguer	2:24
I'm Yours	Isabel LaRosa	2:25
Lil Baby	Mustard, Ty Dolla $ign	4:19
Light Me Up	Ravyn Lenae	3:48
Fire and Light	Actress	1:15
Fine Again	Tirzah	2:53
The Island, Pt. I	Pendulum	5:20
Guttural Sounds	Okay Kaya	3:14
LAY U DOWN/SEXY	Baro Sura	3:45
I'd Love	Auður	3:32
Truth Or Dare	Kelela	4:12
As We Are So Wonderfully Done With Each Other	Kenneth Patchen	1:33
Honey	Raveena	4:31

1h 50m

(Summer '22) [Rewind]

Massive	Drake	5:36
Pour Up	Yaya Bey, DJ Nativesun	2:05
Happy	Ashanti	4:22
Dreams, Fairytales, Fantasies	A$AP Ferg, Brent Faiyaz, Salaam Remi	3:42
Kinda Love	TeaMarrr	3:07
Over the Moon	Asi Kemera	2:04
Empty House	Air	2:58
Untouched	The Veronicas	4:15
Purple Drank	Axel Boman	7:20
La Tortura	Shakira, Alejandro Sanz	3:32
Love Muscle	Honey Dijon, Tim K, Nomi Ruiz	4:49
Fallin'	J. Alphonso Nicholson	2:48
Ignite Dat Ass on Fire	Reon Vangèr	3:57
Got to Be Real	Cheryl Lynn	5:07
Taste Your Love	Horace Brown, Tyme	4:46
Sweet Honey	Peyton	2:47
Pussy Poppin (I Don't Really Talk Like This)	Rico Nasty	1:56
Liquid Love	Roy Ayers, Sylvia Cox	4:46
Summer	Marshmello	3:53
Precious Possession	Anna Wise	3:46
Wetter	Twista, Erika Shevon	4:16
Oui	Jeremih	3:58
IT WAS MEANT 2 B	KAYTRANADA	4:00
Feel The Breeze	Flwr Chyld, Nai Br.XX	2:51
Gravity	Ferdous	2:38
Lonely Nights	LEISURE	3:20
Rewind	Kelela	3:58
I Think That I Love You	Zyah Belle, ROMderful	4:14
Whipped Cream Daydream	Tunde Olaniran, Ah-Mer-Ah-Su	2:57
Kiss Me	Cassie	4:07
Vibrations	070 Shake	3:41

1h 57m

(Eros) [Paris]

Pressure	Martin Garrix, Tove Lo	2:23
Sexual	NEIKED, Dyo	3:08
Once I Was	Tim Buckley	3:22
Multi-Love	Unknown Mortal Orchestra	4:10
I Miss You (Dobie Rub Part One) - Sunshine Mix	Björk, Dobie	5:35
The First Time Ever I Saw Your Face	Marcia Griffiths	4:10
Feu de camp	Lymass	1:24
Fallin' High	Safri Duo	5:57
Have You Been Good to Yourself	Johnnie Frierson	3:48
Les amants	Les Rita Mitsouko	5:18
Hard Rain	Lykke Li	3:30
Dreams Fall	Kindness	4:28
Venus As a Boy	Vitamin String Quartet	2:53
Eye of the Tiger	Survivor	4:03
Gun In My Hand	Dorothy	3:19
Flower	Liz Phair	2:02
Coin-operated Boy	The Dresden Dolls	4:45
Astronaut In The Ocean	Masked Wolf	2:12
Sketch For Summer	The Durutti Column	2:30
A Mask of My Own Face	Lemon Demon	3:30
Violin	Cookiee Kawaii, Dear Silas	1:49
Breath Control	Recoil	6:42
Think Harder	StreamBeats by Harris Heller	2:07
Blood in the Water	Oh He Dead	2:47
Let X=X	Laurie Anderson	3:54
It Tango	Laurie Anderson	3:01
Paris (Aeroplane Remix)	**Friendly Fires, Aeroplane**	**7:45**
I Need Somebody To Love Tonight	Sylvester	6:50
Just Can't Get Enough	Depeche Mode	3:42
One Kiss	Tess Gallagher	1:54
I See You	Little Simz	3:58

1h 57m

(Selene) [Moonlight]

Sound & Color	Alabama Shakes	3:02
Hymn For Her	Anchor & Braille	5:05
Everything In Its Right Place	Radiohead	4:11
The Weight	Amber Run	4:07
Witchcraft	Frank Sinatra	2:53
Nice To Have	070 Shake	3:52
Nice To Have - Instrumental	070 Shake	3:56
MY POWER	Nija, Beyoncé, Busiswa, et al	4:20
Lavender	Copeland	4:11
Lava	Alkistis Protopsalti	4:55
Silhouette	Aquilo	3:50
Oh No!!!	WILLOW	3:10
Cave Ballad	Andy Hull, ADONIS McDowell, et al	1:45
Holy Ghost	BØRNS	4:16
Moondust - Stripped	Jaymes Young	3:36
Stupid Deep - Acoustic	Jon Bellion	2:39
Ilomilo	Billie Eilish	2:36
Die Trying	Michl	3:29
A Restless Night	Dario Marianelli, Jack Liebeck, et al	1:59
I Found	Amber Run	4:33
Ungodly Hour	Chloe x Halle	4:15
Venus	Sleeping At Last	3:20
Venus - Instrumental	Sleeping At Last	3:20
Residue	Tayla Parx	2:26
Never Ending Circles	CHVRCHES	3:06
Under The Moon	070 Shake	3:27
MOONLIGHT	TWICE	3:39
Fuck it I love you	Lana Del Rey	3:38
Hearts A Mess	Gotye	6:05
Friendly Dark	Ollie MN	3:24
Runaway	AURORA	4:08

1h 53m

(Summer Renaissance) [Summer '22]

My Universe	Coldplay, BTS	3:46
Sexy Ways	Funkadelic	3:08
Just the Way You Are	Bruno Mars	3:40
SUMMER RENAISSANCE	Beyoncé	4:33
Prosecco	Th&o.	3:41
You're The One (That I Adore) - Single Version	Bobby "Blue" Bland	2:32
Abracadabra	Sean Nicholas Savage	3:52
Can't Get You out of My Head	Kylie Minogue	3:50
Find Me	Manú	3:39
Pame Mia Volta Sto Feggari	Savina Yannatou	4:32
Get Low	Glüme	3:10
Tonight, We Fall	ADULT.	4:25
Goddess	Jaira Burns	3:07
Unchained Melody	The Righteous Brothers	3:38
Happy Together	FLOOR CRY	2:20
Talking Body	Tove Lo	3:58
I Am Your God	MOTHERMARY	4:02
Stay Ready (What A Life)	Jhené Aiko, Kendrick Lamar	6:22
You Put A Spell On Me	Wiild Berry	3:28
Sacrifice	Bebe Rexha	2:40
Gimme Love	Rosenfeld	3:15
Foreign Car	Kelsey Lu	3:17
Woman	Doja Cat	2:52
Swept Away	The xx	4:59
Hypnotic	Zella Day	2:56
Breathe	Parah Dice, Brianna	2:49
Summertime	My Chemical Romance	4:06
I Love You	Goldie Boutilier	5:03
Truth Or Dare	Heaven	2:55
Heart Over Head	Saâda Bonaire	4:38
Kind of Love	Tasha	4:38

1h 56m

(Elegy) [Pearly Gates] —*for Olivia*

Track Of The Cat	Pram	4:13
Six Appeal (My Daddy Rocks Me)	Benny Goodman Sextet, Benny Goodman, Charlie Christian	3:17
Half the Day Is the Night	Gábor Szabó	4:22
Fantas for Saxophone and Voice	Caternia Barbieri, Bendik Giske	7:16
Soundcheck	Chelsey Green and Green Project	3:50
This Life (Instrumental)	Sareem Poems, Newselph	3:20
Ferryboat of the Mind	Clinic	2:09
Solenzara	Omar Khorshid	5:52
An Ending, a Beginning	Dustin O'Halloran	2:08
Promenade	Trigg & Gusset	4:30
Textures	Herbie Hancock	6:38
Falling, Catching	Agnes Obel	1:33
Carry Me Out	Mitski	3:53
Salamatu	Mamman Sani	4:51
Joiwind	Vakula	3:26
Cikmaz Sokak	insanlar gerçek olsa	1:48
Mysterious River Snake	The Sweet Enoughs	2:56
Crockett's Theme	Jan Hammer	3:36
To the Moon	junodream	2:50
Who Does She Hope To Be?	Sonny Sharrock	4:41
Silhouette	Carlton Maison Quartet	3:51
Sweet Eyes	Elias Rahbani	2:41
I Hide Myself Within My Flower	Lena Platonos, Sissi Rada	2:15
Flow	Laurie Anderson	2:14
Bird's Lament	Moondog	2:03
Riders On the Storm	Yonderboi	4:19
Pearly Gates	**Grimez**	**3:29**
What You Love You Must Love Now	The Six Parts Seven	5:22
Champagne Poetry (Instrumental)	Instrumental Trap Beats Gang	2:24
Kiss of The Phoenix	Eartheater	3:03
Images in a Mirror - Stereo	Sun Ra	3:42

1h 52m

(Eternity) [Tokyo]

The Beginning of Memory	Laurie Anderson	2:45
Sexual Hallucination	In This Moment, Brent Smith	6:17
Lay My Love	Brian Eno, John Cale	4:43
Old Man with Young Ideas	Ann Peebles	3:08
Eau D'bedroom Dancing	Le Tigre	2:55
Come Undone	Isobel Campbell, Mark Lanegan	5:43
Spiritual Eternal	Alice Coltrane	2:56
Freedom	Charles Mingus	5:10
Love Walks In	Van Halen	5:10
Poète maudit	Laurie Darmon	3:14
I Love You, I Hate You	Little Simz	4:15
Falling	Julee Cruise	5:21
The Butterfly	Ronn McFarlane	2:31
Walk This Way	Run-D.M.C., Aerosmith	5:10
Bullet With Butterfly Wings	The Smashing Pumpkins	4:18
Lovely Head	Goldfrapp	3:49
Can We Kiss Forever?	Kina, Adriana Proenza	3:07
Oh To Be Opened	vōx	1:03
In Other Worlds	Barry Adamson	3:44
I'm Your Man	Leonard Cohen	4:24
Red Light	Siouxsie and the Banshees	3:21
Only Seeing God When I Come	Sega Bodega	3:20
Moonlight Densetsu - Remix	Patrick Moon Bird	1:57
Japanese Hotel	Blush'ko	3:37
X	Xzibit	4:15
Taste	Rhye	3:45
Tokyo Drift (Fast & Furious)	Teriyaki Boyz	4:14
My Love	Lenny Kravitz	3:52
Beg For You	Charli XCX, Rina Sawayama	2:47
A Kiss To Build A Dream On	Louis Armstrong	3:00
Can't Take My Eyes Off of You	Ms. Lauryn Hill	3:41

1h 57m

(Adonis) [No Limit]

Oslo in the Summertime	of Montreal	3:21
Sex & Sadness	Madi Sipes & The Painted Blue	4:07
Body	Glüme	3:40
My Body Is a Cage	Arcade Fire	4:47
Uh Huh	B2K	3:43
Don't Bring Me Down	Electric Light Orchestra	4:03
Sisyphus	Andrew Bird	4:07
Disturbia	Rihanna	3:58
No Filter	Black Coast, Madison Love	4:03
Sexy Boy	Air	4:58
CHA-CHING	Royal Cinema	2:52
Euphoria	Dianna Lopez	3:59
Mystic Man	Peter Tosh	5:56
You Can't Always Get What You Want	The Rolling Stones	7:28
Even If It Hurts	Tei Shi, Blood Orange	4:11
I'm Not Perfect (But I'm Perfect For You)	Grace Jones	3:58
Altar	Dizzy Fae	3:26
Deep End - Alt Version	Lykke Li	5:33
My Body Hurts	Sofi Tukker	3:03
Maniac	Phoebe Green	3:30
Lavender	Biig Piig	3:11
Fire in My Heart	Escape from New York	5:13
Spying Glass	Horace Andy	5:06
Welcome to the Black Parade	My Chemical Romance	5:11
IT HURTS!	San Holo	3:48
Addicted	One True God	2:42
No Limit	G-Eazy, A$AP Rocky, Cardi B	4:05
And We Hear "I Love You"	Lena Platonos	2:40
On And On	Curtis Harding	4:01
When Doves Cry	Prince	5:52
What Do You Like In Me	Nasty Cherry	3:24

2h 10m

(Désir) [La Fête Noire]

Camino Del Sol	Antena	3:42
Lo Boob Oscillator	Stereolab	6:36
Éternel été	Ezéchiel Pailhès	3:24
La coeur au bout des doigts	Jacqueline Taieb	2:38
Alors on danse - Radio Edit	Stromae	3:26
Sans cesse, mon chéri	Domenique Dumont	4:07
Autopsie d'un complot	Ahmed Malek	3:29
Rien n'est parfait	TAL	3:06
Toi et moi	Guillaume Grand	3:46
Je N'en Connais Pas La Fin -	Jeff Buckley	5:02
Live at Sin-é, NY, NY		
J'sais pas	Johan Papaconstantino	3:18
Voyage voyage	Desireless	4:26
Ya Bismillah	Mamman Sani	4:21
Tous Les Garçons Et Les Filles	Eurythmics, Annie Lennox, Dave Stewart	3:25
Divine idylle	Vanessa Paradis	2:39
Mon amour, mon ami	Marie Laforêt	2:18
Ego - Radio Edit	Willy William	3:27
Résiste	France Gall	4:32
Dépassée par le fantasme	Essaie Pas	5:17
I'm A Lie	Charlotte Gainsbourg	3:29
Polaroid / Roman / Photo	Ruth	5:01
Encore	Vendredi sur Mer	3:16
Comptine d'un autre été, l'après-midi	Yann Tiersen	2:20
Au coin du monde - Streets Go Down	Keren Ann	3:21
Aimer sans amour	Guts	4:17
La décadanse - Bande originale du film	Jane Birkin, Serge Gainsbourg	5:13
"Sex Shop"		
La fête noire	Flavien Berger	6:04
Hymne à l'amour	Édith Piaf	3:25
Ces mots stupides	Sacha Distel, Joanna Shimkus	2:36
Moi...Lolita	Alizée	4:24
Ne me quitte pas	Jacques Brel	3:49

2h

(Room 109) [Estranged]

Heart of the Sunrise	Yes	10:34
I Want Your Sex – Pts. 1&2	George Michael	9:17
Love from Room 109 at the Islander	Tim Buckley	10:49
Station to Station	David Bowie	10:17
Rapper's Delight – Long Version	The Sugarhill Gang	14:33
Voodoo Chile	Jimi Hendrix	14:59
An Analog Guy in a Digital World	Martin Roth	8:46
Grand Cru – Pachanga Boys Glam Drive	Saschienne	13:15
A Change Is Going To Come	Baby Huey	9:31
Hymne à l'Amour	Jeff Buckley, Gary Lucas	11:34
Child in Time	Deep Purple	10:20
The Truth, The Glow, The Fall	Anna von Hausswolff	12:07
Sukothai (1977)	Carl Stone	14:31
I Heard It Through The Grapevine	Creedence Clearwater Revival	11:07
Venice Bitch	Lana Del Rey	9:37
Shine On You Crazy Diamond, Pts. 1-5	Pink Floyd	13:31
Tonight, Tonight, Tonight	Genesis	8:50
Sinnerman	Nina Simone	10:19
Jellyfish Sunrise	Daikaiju	9:55
Nothing Left but Their Names	Kronos Quartet, Laurie Anderson	9:38
Follow Me – Medley	Amanda Lear	19:41
Disco Inferno	The Trammps	10:59
Blue Train – Live in Stockholm, Sweden/1961	John Coltrane	8:55
Under The Pressure	The War On Drugs	8:52
Third Eye Sh*t	Joey Bada$$, PRO ERA, et al	11:46
Welcome To The Pleasuredome	Frankie Goes To Hollywood	13:40
Estranged	Guns N' Roses	9:23
Love To Love You Baby	Donna Summer	16:48
Marquee Moon	Television	10:38
Mother Sky (from Deep End)	CAN	14:31
Duk Koo Kim	Sun Kil Moon	14:32

6h 3m

(Selene) [Unearth Me]

Electric Love - Oliver Remix	BØRNS	4:13
Electricity	Silk City, Dua Lipa, Diplo, et al	3:58
Head On Fire	Griff, King Princess, MØ, Sigrid	3:31
Paradise	Coldplay	4:38
SING	My Chemical Romance	4:30
Earth	Sleeping At Last	4:28
The Cloud Atlas Sextet for Orchestra	Tom Tykwer, Johnny Klimek, et al	4:57
Queen of Your Heart	Tut Tut Child, Augustus Ghost	5:16
Ooh	Jon Bellion, Christianne Jensen	3:39
Wandering Guitar	Ike Reiko	2:43
Spirit Animal	Sleep Thieves	3:13
Violet Hour	Abuja 336, J. Caesar, et al	4:40
Paris	Else	3:29
Rhiannon	Fleetwood Mac	4:12
Wraith Pinned to the Mist and Other Games	of Montreal	4:15
La Vie en rose	Édith Piaf	3:07
Flower Tattoo (Ouri Rework)	Mind Bath, Ouri, Forever	2:57
Take Care of You	Charlotte Day Wilson, King Princess, Amaarae, et al	3:34
Inhale Exhale	Strria	1:25
BREAK MY SOUL	Beyoncé	4:38
Asmr	Only Fire	2:50
Grand Cru	Saschienne	6:22
Tsunami - Blasterjaxx Remix	DVBBS, Borgeous, Blasterjaxx	5:37
Adore You	Harry Styles	3:27
Sweet Spot	Kim Petras	3:14
Voodoo?	L'Impératrice	4:15
Unearth Me	Oklou	3:25
Sea of Love	Cat Power	2:19
Frozen	Sabrina Claudio	4:04
Let Me Adore You	Soko	3:35
Such Great Heights	The Postal Service	4:26

2h 1m

(Atopos) [G.U.Y.]

Roam	The B-52's	4:55
Do It Again	Röyksopp, Robyn	5:06
Bloom	Troye Sivan	3:42
Daddy	Tommy Genesis	2:44
Easy	Sugababes	3:38
Don't It Make My Brown Eyes Blue	Crystal Gayle	2:27
(I Just) Died In Your Arms	Cutting Crew	4:40
Slow	Kylie Minogue	3:13
Down For Whatever	Kelly Rowland, The WAV.s	3:53
Je t'aime moi non plus	Serge Gainsbourg, Jane Birkin	4:28
Sock It 2 Me	Missy Elliott, Da Brat	4:17
I Said Never Again (But Here We Are)	Rachel Stevens	3:25
XO	Beyoncé	3:35
Gimme! Gimme! Gimme! (A Man After Midnight)	ABBA	4:52
Cake By The Ocean	DNCE	3:39
Love Me Harder	Ariana Grande, The Weeknd	3:56
Spider-Man Dick	cupcakKe	3:48
Get Down, Make Love	Queen	3:51
Backdoor Lover	DuJour	3:40
Know You Better	Blush'ko	3:55
Body	070 Shake, Christine and the Queens	3:30
Lavender	Biig Piig	3:11
Sanctify	Years & Years	3:12
I/You	vōx	2:44
1,000,000 X Better	Griff, HONNE	3:11
Dreams and Converse	Dawn Richard	3:17
G.U.Y.	**Lady Gaga**	**3:52**
Whole Lotta Love	Led Zeppelin	5:33
Door of the Cosmos	Sun Ra & His Arkestra	9:00
Melting	Kali Uchis	3:28
Trading Places	Usher	4:28

2h 3m

(Heartbreak) [My Body Left My Soul]

No More Home, No More Love	Soko	2:36
Why Do You Lie To Me	Topic, A7S, Lil Baby	2:51
When You Say My Name	Chandler Leighton	2:28
Baby I'm Dead Inside	KOPPS	3:17
Apogee	Fytch	4:17
I'll Make You Love Me	Kat Leon	3:28
History	070 Shake	4:50
Los Ageless	St. Vincent	4:41
My Body's a Zombie For You	Dead Man's Bones	4:30
Hartino To Feggaraki	Lena Platonos	2:41
Sleeping In Your Garden	Gia Ford	3:24
Never Say Die	CHVRCHES	4:23
Weird Awakenings	L'FREAQ	3:31
Roll Like Thunder	Jake Wells	3:42
Highest Building	Flume, Oklou	3:36
Man On My Mind	Cornelia Murr	3:42
Twist The Knife	Chromatics	3:27
You Know Where My Happiness Went	Valentina	3:22
GONE, GONE/THANK YOU	Tyler, The Creator	6:15
Concealer	Eartheater	2:38
Hide & Seek	Causeway	3:47
Watch Me Burn	Michele Morrone	3:06
Plans We Made	Son Lux	3:40
Sleeping Beauty	Night Things	3:50
Only When I	Alice Phoebe Lou	3:51
Notice Of Eviction	Saul Williams	4:18
My Body Left My Soul	USERx, Matt Maeson, Rozwell, Pusha T	4:20
A Potion For Love	AURORA	3:36
Out My Mind, Just In Time	Erykah Badu	10:21
Caught In Time, So Far Away	You'll Never Get to Heaven	3:48
Bye-bye Darling	BØRNS	4:59

2h 3m

(Euphoria) [Won't]

Innerbloom – What So Not Remix	RÜFÜS DU SOL, What So Not	4:37
Teenage Blue	Dreamgirl	3:54
Always Forever	Cults	3:43
Blood In the Wine	AURORA	3:29
Super Stars	Yves Tumor	3:05
CUFF IT	Beyoncé	3:45
Witches	Alice Phoebe Lou	3:15
HEARTBEAT	Isabel LaRosa	2:04
My Consequence	Hey Violet	4:22
Ayrilik Olsa Bile	Esmeray	3:10
You Are Enough	Sleeping At Last	3:00
On Air	What So Not, Louis The Child, Captain Cuts, JRM	3:57
Myth	Beach House	4:18
Thank You	Amber Run	3:30
Till Death Do Us Part	Rosenfeld	3:24
Gladly	Tirzah	3:41
Big Jet Plane	Angus & Julia Stone	3:59
Euphor	Novo Amor, Ed Tullett, Lowswimmer	4:03
It Won't Stop	Sevyn Streeter, Chris Brown	4:41
W.I.T.C.H.	Devon Cole	2:12
Only Angel	Harry Styles	4:51
Outta My Head	Tropic Gold	3:38
Let Me Follow	Son Lux	4:48
Song For You	Rhye	3:58
Whenever Wherever Whatever	Maxwell	3:45
Hunnybee	Unknown Mortal Orchestra	4:28
Won't	Tanerélle	4:03
Damned to Love You	Miserable	3:24
Serenade of Water	Men I Trust	3:05
But You	Alexandra Savior	2:53
See You in the Dark – From "Little Fish"	Soko, Keegan DeWitt	3:21

1h 54m

(Kink) [Daddy]

Call Me Daddy	11:11	2:48
Sad Sex	Ängie, Tail Whip	3:25
BABYDOLL	Ari Abdul	3:16
Milk	Allie X	3:30
Skin	Mac Miller	4:47
Blue Moon Motel	Nicole Dollanganger	2:55
Do It for Me	Rosenfeld	3:22
Spinning Over You	REYKO	3:14
Catching Feels	ppcocaine	3:15
F*ck Me & Feed Me	Rendezvous At Two	3:28
I Wanna Be Yours	Arctic Monkeys	3:03
High For This	The Weeknd	4:09
Suck It and See	Arctic Monkeys	3:45
Oh Daddy	Fleetwood Mac	3:56
Lolita	Knee High Fox	2:25
Big Bad Handsome Man	Imelda May	2:43
Hey There Cowgirl	Palm Springsteen	3:38
Wrap Me In Plastic	CHROMANCE, Marcus Layton	3:13
34+35	Ariana Grande	2:53
Tag, You're It	Melanie Martinez	3:09
Shakin' It 4 Daddy	Robin Thicke, Nicki Minaj	3:51
You Can Be The Boss	SirLofi	3:04
Gangsta	Kehlani	2:57
Girls Your Age	Transviolet	3:28
Guys My Age	Hey Violet	3:33
Use Me	PVRIS, 070 Shake	3:23
Daddy	**SAKIMA, ylxr**	**2:32**
70's Porno Music	Cute Whore	2:30
Smells Like Sex	Sizzy Rocket	1:57
Holy	Zolita	3:02
Bad Girl	Avril Lavigne, Marilyn Manson	2:54

1h 40m

(Kink) [Daddy AF]

Daddy	Die Antwoord	3:59
SEX MED DIN DADDY	Rasmus Gozzi, JeppsoN, et al	2:26
I'm His Girl	Friends	2:52
DDLG	ppcocaine	2:35
Talk to My Skin	Stalgia	3:40
Knee Socks	Arctic Monkeys	4:17
Daddy Cool	Boney M.	3:28
Senpai	Shiki-TMNS, Hentai Dude	2:52
Beggin'	Måneskin	3:31
Bonita	Isabel	3:25
Daddy Loves You	Dana Dentata	2:21
Use Me	Makk Mikkael	3:13
Boss	Ängie	3:08
Cola	Lana Del Rey	4:20
White Icing	Cute Whore	3:50
Daddy! Daddy! Do!	AmaLee	4:11
BDE	Shygirl, slowthai	2:48
Keep It Down	Migrant Motel	2:44
Every Baby Needs A Da-Da Daddy	Kate Michaels	3:05
I KNOW WHAT U LIKE	Sizzy Rocket, chloe mk	2:47
BOMBÓN	Daddy Yankee, El Alfa, Lil Jon	3:02
Bathroom Bitch	HOLYCHILD	2:49
Cosmic	chloe mk	3:00
Love Surrounds You	Ramsey	3:19
Lollipop (Yum bi dum like Bubblegum)	CHROMANCE	3:00
Toxic	2WEI	3:57
Daddy AF	**Slayyyter**	**2:31**
Loving You	Rendezvous At Two	3:22
Comfort	Pour Vous	2:53
Kiss Me In Slow Motion	Ängie	3:15
Siren	Kailee Morgue	3:20

1h 40m

(Death) [Faith Consuming Hope]

I Heard a Sigh	Cortex	3:29
Death By Sex	Kim Petras	3:22
All Rights Reserved	The Chemical Brothers	4:42
10,000 Emerald Pools	BØRNS	2:54
New Love Cassette	Angel Olsen	3:26
Last Night	Arooj Aftab	5:58
Scratch Walking	Lee "Scratch" Perry	3:07
River	Bishop Briggs	3:36
A Comma	serpentwithfeet	2:47
Voilà	Françoise Hardy	3:22
The Great Hope Design	Sevdaliza	5:20
Turned Out I Was Everyone	SASAMI	4:59
Mystery of Love	Mr. Fingers	7:10
Back To Life	Soul II Soul, Caron Wheeler	3:48
Home	Just Jinjer	3:44
My Manic And I	Laura Marling	3:56
Set The Controls For The Heart Of The Pelvis	Barry Adamson, Jarvis Cocker	5:39
Momamma Scuba	John Cale	4:24
Myself When I Am Real	Charles Mingus	7:35
When I R.I.P.	Labrinth	2:54
Comme Des Garçons	Rina Sawayama	3:01
Mirrored Heart	FKA twigs	4:32
Outside the Gate (for Bruna)	Anna von Hausswolff	5:23
I've Never Been So Happy To Be Bleeding	vōx	2:28
Sex is good (but have you tried)	Donna Missal	3:35
Euphoria	Dianna Lopez	4:00
Faith Consuming Hope	Eartheater	4:50
Lover, Please Stay - Live	Nothing But Thieves	3:40
Mouthful of Diamonds	Phantogram	4:13
Body	Gia Margaret	2:19
Weakness	Prismo	3:17

2h 7m

(Slow Jams) [In the Dark]

Feels Like This	Abra Taylor	3:15
Sapiosex	Micky Weekes	2:35
DDLG	Katerina May	2:18
So Good	Warpaint	5:59
Sweet Takeover	Pointe Claire	3:50
Play With Me	Rendezvous At Two	4:12
Bedspell	Zolita	2:49
GITY	Chymes	2:51
What You Like	Aliek	3:14
I Wanna Know	Joe	4:56
Don't You Know	Jaymes Young	4:08
Heartbeats - Radio Version	Ah-Mer-Ah-Su, davOmakesbeats	3:03
You Think I'm Horny	Desire Marea	4:07
So Damn Into You	Vlad Holiday	4:12
I Want It	Two Feet	2:19
You're so Cool	Nicole Dollanganger	4:15
Lion	Saint Mesa	2:50
I Won't Let You Down	Curtis Harding	4:04
You're All I Want	Cigarettes After Sex	4:24
Through Eyes and Glass	Ann Wilson & The Daybreaks	3:19
Siren	Tanerélle	3:16
Like I'm Winning It	Girlpool	3:16
A Pill to Crush	Evalyn	3:41
Ache	FKA twigs	5:00
Together	The xx	5:25
Addict	Tei Shi	3:26
SLOW JAMS IN THE DARK	Xoxocouron	**2:51**
Found Love	Sofya Wang	2:43
All I Really Want Is You	The Marias	3:11
Kissin' You	Total	4:42
Our Song	The xx	3:13

1h 54m

(Human Face) [London]

Space Flight	I-Roy	3:13
Sexual (Li Da Di) – Thunderpuss Remix	Amber, Thunderpuss	3:46
My Name Is Trouble	Keren Ann	4:13
Your Body Changes Everything	Perfume Genius, Boy Harsher	5:06
Nite Life	ADULT.	4:43
Hallelu Ya Hallelu Me	Okay Kaya	2:46
An Amalgamation Waltz 1839	Joep Beving	4:06
Pynk - King Topher Remix	Janelle Monáe, Grimes, King Topher	3:58
Doctor Robert	The Beatles	2:14
I'd Like To Walk Around In Your Mind	Vashti Bunyan	2:15
(To me) your face is love	Donna Missal	3:36
Love & Validation - Single Edit	Boys Noize, Kelsey Lu	4:00
Now, Voyager	Charles Gerhardt	5:52
Straight to Hell	The Clash	5:30
The Other Side of Paradise	Glass Animals	5:20
FACE	BROCKHAMPTON	4:19
You're Too Precious	James Blake	3:43
Guns of Brixton	Nouvelle Vague, Camille	4:06
Lullaby for Realville	Sun Ra	4:47
(A) Face in the Crowd	The Kinks	2:19
TO THE MOON	Jnr Choi, Sam Tompkins	2:32
Coming	David Motion, Sally Potter, et al	6:03
6 Encores for Piano: No. 3, Wasserklavier	Marino Formenti	2:19
The Wind	PJ Harvey	4:01
Quicksand - Standard Version	La Roux	3:05
Who Wants To Live Forever	Queen	5:15
Hallelujah - Live in London	Leonard Cohen	7:20
Past Lives	BØRNS	4:34
Human	Rag'n'Bone Man	3:20
The Pure and the Damned	Oneohtrix Point Never, Iggy Pop	4:29
Death of a Party	Blur	4:33

2h 7m

(The Club) [Rack City]

Baby Wyd?	Nardo Wick, Lakeyah	2:54
Sexual	Dave East, Chris Brown	3:40
It's A Vibe	2 Chainz, Ty Dolla $ign, Trey Songz, Jhené Aiko	3:29
Hot In Herre	Nelly	3:47
Novacane	Frank Ocean	5:01
Thong Song	Sisqó	4:13
Mystery of Love - Mixed	Mr. Fingers	2:32
S&M	Rihanna	4:03
Bust a Move	Young MC	4:23
WAP	Cardi B, Megan Thee Stallion	3:06
Get Low	Lil Jon & The East Side Boyz	5:33
Round of Applause	Waka Flocka Flame, Drake	4:25
Tokyo Drift (trap bass)	Trap Remix Guys	4:05
Baby Got Back	Sir Mix-A-Lot	4:21
XXXTC	Brooke Candy, Charli XCX, Maliibu Miitch	3:17
DOLLAZ ON MY HEAD	Gunna, Young Thug	3:17
Lollipop	Lil Wayne, Static Major	4:59
Moonlight	XXXTENTACION	2:14
Rated X	Miles Davis	6:50
Mask Off	Future	3:24
Bandz A Make Her Dance	Juicy J, Lil Wayne, 2 Chainz	4:38
Intercourse	Megan Thee Stallion, Mustard, Popcaan	3:16
Astronomia	Vicetone, Tony Igy	3:17
Poison	Bell Biv DeVoe	4:21
X	ScHoolboy Q, 2 Chainz, Saudi	4:27
Pop That	French Montana, Rick Ross, Drake, Lil Wayne	5:03
Rack City	Tyga	3:22
I Luv Dem Strippers	2 Chainz, Nicki Minaj	3:59
Juicy	Young Dolph	3:12
Standing Ovation	Paper Route EMPIRE, Big Moochie Grape	2:59
Back That Azz Up	Juvenile, Lil Wayne, Mannie Fresh	3:05

2h 3m

(Reverie) [Los Angeles]

Beautiful	Goldfrapp	4:49
Sexual Eruption	Snoop Dogg	4:00
Who I Am	Toro y Moi	3:28
California Love	2Pac, Roger, Dr. Dre	4:44
The Book Lovers	Broadcast	4:49
Angel	Kali Uchis	2:22
Requiem For A Father	The Durutti Column	5:07
Do It To It	ACRAZE, Cherish	2:37
Strawberry Letter 23	Shuggie Otis	3:59
Cybele's Reverie	Stereolab	4:42
Nobody Sees Me Like You Do	Yoko Ono, The Apples In Stereo	3:55
Female Energy, Part 2	WILLOW	2:53
Pacific Coast Highway	Fukkk Offf	3:24
Welcome To The Jungle	Guns N' Roses	4:33
Oblivion	Grimes	4:10
Love Again	Dua Lipa	4:17
Hit It Hard	Peaches	3:25
California Shake	Margo Guryan	3:28
Digital Versicolor	Glass Candy	5:57
Poker Face	Lady Gaga	3:56
Body Move	Dizzy Fae	2:56
Cum	Brooke Candy, Iggy Azalea	2:37
Pearly Gates Smoke Machine	Guided By Voices	4:01
Swim Good	vōx	3:24
X	Tinsahe, Jeremih	2:50
No Tomorrow	Le Matos, PAWWS	4:31
Los Angeles	The Midnight	6:28
Let's Make Love and Listen to Death	CSS	3:30
Feel Your Weight - Poolside Remix	Rhye, Poolside	5:09
I Was Made For Lovin' You	KISS	4:30
Wired	Sonny Fodera, Ella Eyre	3:22

2h 5m

(Elon Musk) [Moon Awaits]

Blame It on Your Love	Charli XCX, Lizzo	3:11
Sex (I'm A...)	Berlin	5:08
Why Don't You Eat Me Now, You Can	Soko	1:28
Heavy Voodoo	Lee "Scratch" Perry	5:03
Lyrics to Go	A Tribe Called Quest	4:09
(They Long To Be) Close To You	Carpenters	4:36
Miles Runs the Voodoo Down	Miles Davis, Wayne Shorter, et al	14:01
Sade In The 90s	Qveen Herby	3:40
Do My Thing	Erika de Casier	3:46
Paper Thin Hotel	Matt Maltese	4:26
They Say I'm Different	Betty Davis	4:15
Breaking Me	Topic, A7S	2:46
An Analog Guy in a Digital World	Martin Roth	8:47
Some Velvet Morning	Nancy Sinatra, Lee Hazlewood	3:41
A Little More	Machine Gun Kelly, Victoria Monét	3:57
Voodoo Child (Slight Return)	Jimi Hendrix	5:13
Hypnotize	The Notorious B.I.G.	3:49
Frank Sinatra	Miss Kittin, The Hacker	3:55
Freedom of Speech	Drauf & Dran	6:50
For The Night	Pop Smoke, Lil Baby, DaBaby	3:10
Savior	St. Vincent	3:26
Fear	Seratones	3:34
Unhealthy Bias	StreamBeats by Harris Heller	2:10
I Was A Window	SASAMI, Dustin Payseur	3:34
Look Who's Cryin' Now	Jessie Murph	2:21
Pursuit of Happiness (Nightmare)	Kid Cudi, MGMT, Ratatat	4:55
Moon Awaits	Beazzo	3:12
Who Lives, Who Dies, Who Tells Your Story	Original Broadway Cast of Hamilton	3:37
Silence	The Golden Filter	6:44
The Best Love Poem I Can Write at the Moment	Charles Bukowski	3:21
The Sound Mirror	Sun Ra & His Arkestra	9:07

2h 22m

(Greatest Love) [Can't Get Enough]

Love Of My Life (An Ode To Hip Hop)	Erykah Badu, Common	5:37
Sexy Love	Ne-Yo	3:40
Lovesong	The Cure	3:28
(Everything I Do) I Do It For You	Bryan Adams	6:34
Ethereal	Audent	4:26
LOVE.	Kendrick Lamar, Zacari	3:33
Mercury	Sleeping At Last	3:33
Body Talk	Imagination	6:08
Love of My Life	Carlos Santana, Dave Matthews, Carter Beauford	5:47
Efecto	Bad Bunny	3:33
You Know How to Make Me Happy	HTRK	3:47
Here With Me	Marshmello, CHVRCHES	2:36
Your Love Is King	Sade	3:39
The Power Of Love	Huey Lewis & The News	3:54
The Sweetest Thing (I've Ever Known)	Juice Newton	4:07
Greatestlove	Musiq Soulchild	4:45
Make Me Feel	Janelle Monáe	3:14
Young And Beautiful	Lana Del Rey	3:56
Wild Love	Cashmere Cat, The Weeknd, Francis and the Lights	3:27
Never Tear Us Apart	INXS	3:05
Love Your Body	Cookiee Kawaii, Oya Noire	2:58
Smoke – Son Lux Remix	BOBI ANDONOV, Son Lux	3:37
THINKING OF U	ABRA	4:46
Like A Star	Corinne Bailey Rae	4:03
I Found You	benny blanco, Calvin Harris	3:09
Demolition Lovers	My Chemical Romance	6:06
Can't Get Enough	Kat Leon, NOCTURN	4:16
I Love You	Karriem	6:55
All of Me	John Legend	4:29
Nothing's Gonna Hurt You Baby	Cigarettes After Sex	4:46
Mirrors	Justin Timberlake	8:04

2h 16m

(Selene) [Sunflower]

Blinding Lights	The Weeknd	3:20
Dreamland	Glass Animals	3:23
Mine	Bazzi	2:11
Overwhelming	Jon Bellion	2:52
If I Tremble	Front Porch Step	4:06
Bloom - Bonus Track	The Paper Kites	3:30
Intro	R A Y	2:07
Runaway (U & I)	Galantis	3:47
I'm Not Rich	The King's Son, Shaggy, et al	3:01
Tout l'univers	Gjon's Tears	3:03
The Louvre	Lorde	4:31
Fallin' (Adrenaline)	Why Don't We	3:36
Eight (Instrumental)	Sleeping At Last	4:10
Take on Me	a-ha	3:45
Heroes (we could be)	Alesso, Tove Lo	3:30
Clouds	BØRNS	3:10
Peaches	In the Valley Below	4:45
Carry Your Throne	Jon Bellion	3:23
Not In Blood, But In Bond	Hans Zimmer	2:13
Happiest Year - Prince Fox Remix	Jaymes Young, Prince Fox	2:35
I WANNA BE YOUR SLAVE	Måneskin	2:53
Summertime In Paris	Jaden, WILLOW	4:30
Light Through a Canvas	Robot Koch, Savannah Jo Lack, et al	4:49
Ocean Eyes	Billie Eilish	3:20
WATER	Salatiel, Pharrel Williams, et al	2:33
Until We Go Down	Ruelle	4:11
Sunflower - Spiderman: Into the Spider-Verse	Post Malone, Swae Lee	2:38
In the Name of Love	Martin Garrix, Bebe Rexha	3:15
Overjoyed	Bastille	3:26
All I Want Is You	Barry Louis Polisar	2:37
Forever	Addal, Cozy	3:33

1h 44m

(Kink) [See You Bleed]

Perverted	Elita	3:08
Sex	JVLA	2:37
Touch You Where It Hurts	Goldilox	3:59
KILL4ME	Marilyn Manson	3:59
Howl	Alexandra Savior	3:08
Shut Up and Listen	Nicholas Bonnin, Angelicca	4:03
This Killing Floor	Talia Stewart	2:14
E-GIRLS ARE RUINING MY LIFE	CORPSE, Savage Ga$p	1:45
Squeeze	Ghostemane	2:20
Shut Me Up	Alexis Munroe	1:51
Silly Putty	phem	2:46
Rabbit Hole	Cherry Glazerr	2:59
Beautiful Mayhem	DeathbyRomy	3:09
Desire	Meg Myers	4:44
SUFFER AND SWALLOW	Alice Glass	2:53
Hurt Me Harder	Zolita	3:00
Destroy Destroy Destroy	Transviolet	3:51
RUNAWAY	REI AMI	2:44
Massacre	Kim Petras	3:26
Lose My Breath	Rhea Robertson	2:03
Bound	Indiana	3:44
Push	Starbenders	2:57
True Love Is Violent	Allie X	3:32
Lil blood	Dana Dentata	2:01
IN MY MOUTH	Black Dresses	3:03
I Feel Like A God	DeathbyRomy	2:59
See You Bleed	Ramsey	3:34
When We	Tank	5:09
Hit Me Right	Johnny Goth	2:48
Posing In Bondage	Japanese Breakfast	4:04
Pray	MOTHERMARY	3:28

1h 38 m

(Counterfactuals) [Lima]

Bouncin	Kiana Ledé, Offset	2:52
Sexual Healing	Marvin Gaye	3:58
Dare To Fly	Sampa the Great, Ecca Vandal	4:22
More Women	Saâda Bonaire	5:10
Messages from the Stars	The Rah Band	7:40
Every Time He Comes Around	Minnie Riperton	3:54
Feu noir	Luc Renot	2:12
Nightclubbing	Grace Jones	5:07
LIFE IS CHANGING	DESTIN CONRAD	3:31
Recuerdos de una Noche	Los Pasteles Verdes	3:02
This Trumpet in My Head	Lykke Li	1:42
Angel Falls	Frank Walker, Sterling Fox	3:57
Burlesque	W&Whale	2:01
Like a Prayer	Madonna	5:40
Bulletproof	La Roux, GAMPER & DADONI	2:42
Your Love Is My Drug	Kesha	3:07
Tent In Your Pants	Peaches	2:52
Try Me On...I'm Very You	Deee-Lite	5:18
The Enchanted Sea	Martin Denny	2:01
Pussy Mask	Peaches	3:15
Come Meh Way	Sudan Archives	2:26
Innocence Is Kinky	Jenny Hval	4:26
I Found The End	Broadcast	2:05
Lonely Sometimes	Oh He Dead	3:03
Is That All There Is?	Cristina	5:43
Disco Clone	Cristina	4:09
La Flor de Canela	Chabuca Granda	3:20
It Takes A Muscle [To Fall In Love]	Spectral Display	3:30
Love Hangover	Diana Ross	7:48
Kiss, Kiss, Kiss	Yoko Ono, Peaches	3:18
Peru	Fireboy DML	2:31

1h 56m

(Love) [Cinematic Love]

Moon Rider	Jai Wolf, Wrabel	3:38
You Got Me Like	SHAED, snny	3:20
Love nwantiti (ah ah ah)	CKay	2:25
Lavender and Velvet	Alina Baraz	3:48
Acoustic	Billy Raffoul	2:52
You You You You You	The 6ths, Katharine Whalen	3:10
Interlude - The Trio	Lana Del Ray	1:15
MIDDLE OF THE NIGHT	Elley Duhé	3:04
P$$Y Fairy (OTW)*	Jhené Aiko	3:01
Ai ga bani	Ali Farka Touré, Toumani Diabaté	4:31
I Hid in Him	vōx	3:05
All the Way Down	Kelela	4:28
Gemini	Desired	1:09
Cherish the Day	Sade	5:32
Ice	alali	3:32
I Get to Love You	Ruelle	3:59
You Know How to Love Me	Phyllis Hyman	7:32
F.ck Me Eyes	Dounia	3:46
It Looks Like Love	Goody Goody	6:23
Strange Effect	Unloved, Raven Violet	2:41
Love Chained	Cannons	3:24
Breatlhess	Caroline Polachek	3:02
Talking to the Moon (Outro)	Jess Benko	1:50
Head First – Young Bombs Remix	Christian French, Young Bombs	3:42
Like a Heartbeat	Blush'ko	3:16
You Are in My System	The System	5:57
Cinematic Love	DSRT, BELLSAINT	3:40
Lovin' you	Tanerélle	4:24
When I Close My Eyes	Shanice	3:22
Ride the dragon	FKA twigs	3:08
Moonlight	Kranium	3:57

1h 53m

(Ο Κόσμος) [L'importante è Finire]

Trema La Terra	Lucilla Galeazzi	4:01
Motel Afrodite	Marília Mendonça, Maiara & Maraisa	2:50
Intazirne	Issam Hajali	3:13
Les Aventures de TINTIN	Taeko Onuki	4:36
Adieu Au Dancefloor	Marie Davidson	5:58
Aaj Shanibar	Rupa	7:59
Unutama Beni	Esmeray	4:07
Ana Yalli Bhebbak	Nancy Ajram	3:28
O Adonis	Alkistis Protopsalti	3:00
Nomalizo	Letta Mbulu	5:11
Hakime Nesh	Tamrat Desta	4:45
Sleepwalking Through the Mekong	Dengue Fever	3:38
Monsieur le Maire de Niafunké	Ali Farka Touré, Toumani Diabaté	3:55
Dragostea Din Tei	O-Zone	3:33
Mariposa Traicionera	Maná	4:24
Sweet On You	Teresa Teng	3:28
Bonbon	Era Istrefi	2:47
Haditouni (Habibi Funk 015)	Douaa	3:25
Funeral Do Lavrador (Funeral of a Worker)	Zelia Barbosa	1:59
Mascarade	YEИDRY, Lous and The Yakuza	2:35
Çayelinden Öteye/Yali Yali	Neşe Karaböcek	2:41
Shinzo No Tobira	Mariah	4:42
Write This Down (Instrumental)	SoulChef	3:08
Jean Genet	Les Hommes Sauvages	3:36
Lo Llaman el Matador	Cacho Castaña	3:04
Plak Plak	IC3PEAK	3:23
L'importante è finire	Mina	3:19
Ti Ein Afto Pou to Lene Agapi	Sophia Loren, Tonis Maroudas	2:26
Macho	Jaakko Eino Kalevi	4:05
Your Dream	Kim Jung Mi	5:26
Mundian to Bach Ke	Panjabi MC	4:04

1h 59m

(Whirlwind) [Don't Despair]

I Woke Up And The Storm Was Over	Tropic of Cancer	7:01
Immortality	Ana Roxanne	4:04
Forgotten, Fossilized, Archaic	Autumn's Grey Solace	4:43
Echo's Answer	Broadcast	3:12
Too Many Voices	Andy Stott	6:07
Keep Driving	Boy Harsher	3:31
Walzer für Robert	Anne Müller	4:11
Genesis	Grimes	4:15
Feeling Dizzy	Everything But The Girl	4:14
Al oeste	Juana Molina	3:37
Unearth	Tsunaina	3:51
Angel Path	Eartheater, LEYA	4:10
A Vampire's Heart	Peter Gundry	2:49
Let It Happen	Tame Impala	7:47
Chrysalis	Pram	3:57
Hierophant	King Woman	7:59
Control	Pleasure Symbols	4:08
Drowning the Call	Mirrorring	6:53
Here Comes The Black Moon	Valium Aggelein	7:26
Secrets	The Bilinda Butchers	5:36
10:37	Beach House	3:48
Come Softly – For Daniel D.	Grouper	4:33
Invitation to the Voyage	Julia Kent	5:29
Darling Effect	Insides	5:03
A Change Of Sex	David Motion, Sally Potter	1:44
Magnificent Oblivion	Fleeting Joys	5:35
Don't Despair	Lafawndah	5:32
Love from NGC 7318	Barnes Blvd., Tanerélle	2:48
Get Free	Lana Del rey	5:34
Blue Madonna	BØRNS	2:19
Tonight Tonight	Celeste	3:39

2h 25m

(Dream) [Altered Reality]

Those Eyes, That Mouth	Cocteau Twins	3:38
Pretty Sexual	Dreamgirl	3:22
Close To You	Dreezy, T-Pain	4:49
This Could Be A Dream	AURORA	4:08
Hymn for the Weekend	Coldplay, Beyoncé	4:18
I'm Waiting Here – Bonus Track	David Lynch, Lykke Li	5:02
December 13, 2017: Geminid Meteor Shower	Sleeping At Last	3:33
You Got the Stuff	Bill Withers	7:14
Young Girl	Don Carlos	3:25
Kaät	Roseaux, Blick Bassy	4:07
Kerosene!	Yves Tumor	5:05
Walking On A Dream	Empire of the Sun	3:18
July 27, 2018: Total Lunar Eclipse	Sleeping At Last	1:42
Hungry Like the Wolf	Duran Duran	3:40
Tastes So Good	Sabrina Claudio	3:06
I Only Have Eyes for You	The Flamingos	3:22
Fantasy	Alina Baraz, Galimatias	3:38
Cocoon	Björk	4:28
January 30, 2020: Spitzer – Final Voyage	Sleeping At Last	2:53
Yin to Yang	runo plum	3:30
You	Snoh Aalegra	3:24
Diamonds	Rihanna	3:45
December 25, 2021: Webb Space Telescope – Launch	Sleeping At Last	3:24
Dreamboat	Joviale	4:28
In Sound, We Found Each Other	Sweet Trip	4:32
Come And Play In The Milky Night	Stereolab	4:38
Altered Reality	DreamWeaver, botanical anomaly	3:25
Lovesick	Alice Phoebe Lou	4:13
I Could Write A Book	Dinah Washington	4:27
Lipstick Stains	Jay Som	1:51
River Rocket	Andy Hull, Robert McDowell, Daniel Radcliffe, Paul Dano	1:57

1h 58m

A RECKONING

HALL

OF

HALL

HALL

HALL

If I Could Find You (Eternity) | The Holydrug Couple

MIRRORS

HALL

MIRRORS

MIRRORS

Skyline with Bridge

I learn the body as desire
from my mother   when I glimpse her nakedness

I learn the body as sublime
from Selene   when I affix my gaze/touch/writing

I live through the longest year with her
dreams falling into life   coming together in playlists

I lose control, I gain heartache
I see my deceit as a kind gesture   and she reciprocates

I call it intimacy, then love, she calls it honest
It grows a scab, I call it new   my heart

She keeps track of the new moon and meteor showers
I don't recognize this act   falling/flying

Cormorant, I feel the air/water
wrapping me in a cocoon   no, a coffin

Caterpillar the heart
Verrazano of the mind   'Is there anything you don't make heavy?'

I say ok, I believe you, even though I don't
because I want to keep fucking   oh, the cock

the mouth, the fenced dream of departure
Some other year I might've climbed down   ha!
                                                ah,
                                              me

INDEX OF SCENES

the stage | Shura

(Adonis falling)

ADONIS: The poems are fictions, except the ones that are true. (Splat!)

DEVIL: Life is a lie, except the parts that are art. (The water is barely disturbed.)

NICO: (Painting) Crystalline...

THAÏS: (Planting) A tiny coffin...

GOD: (Laughing) Adoni...

SELENE: (Pleading) Don't go...

TWO BEASTS: (Plowing) I'm coming! I'm coming!

CHORUS: (All at once) Come. Grieve. Jump. Don't. No. Fuck. You. God. Oh. Selene. Nico. Thaïs. Mom. Mama. Papa. Child. (Sirens) (Horns) (Tires screeching) (Cars colliding) (Wailing) (Coughing) (Gasping) (Birds chirping "Eevee! Eevee!")

Adonis (Modus Operandi)

Start Over Again | Cookiee Kawaii

No, I don't love the idea of you
I love the idea of suicide

One I can wake up from
Suicide as a journey I come back from

Being with you is a form of suicide
A room I step into and emerge from altered

Somewhere else
Non-linear

Purgatory less a test and more an event
A falling away from and a falling into

Skyscraper
Sinkhole

There are only two moments in this imagining
The first is the drop (falling)

My stomach rises to my throat
The second a settling into (melting)

I inhabit these two moments infinitely
Cyclically

I fear the smashing into—
Floor of answers and guts

I'm a dreamer (too lofty)
Or a grinder (I risk too little)

So, no, I don't love the idea of you
I love fucking you

In fucking, there is falling
And melting

Your body carries me into a glare
I brush the horizon

I emerge depleted
And this depletion defines me

As human (alive)
And non-human (resurrected)

You receive payment
As pilot to my journey

To love the idea of a pilot is
To love the idea of a God

So, no, I don't love the idea of you
But I need your body

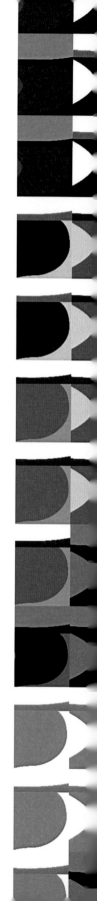

WE NEED A BIGGER COFFIN

Cupid De Locke | **The Smashing Pumpkins**

ADONIS: Why are we not having sex?

SELENE: Because I'm too tired from fucking other guys.

ADONIS: Why are we not having sex?

SELENE: Because I'm too stressed out about my college loans.

ADONIS: Why are we not having sex?

SELENE: Because I'm mad at you for being married.

ADONIS: But why are we not having sex, really?

SELENE: Because I have chlamydia from fucking other guys.

ADONIS: Why are we not having sex?

SELENE: Because my roommate is a self-centered, entitled bitch!

ADONIS: Why are we not having sex?

SELENE: Because I have sexual trauma.

ADONIS: (Deflated)

SELENE: Because I have depression.

ADONIS: I still want you.

SELENE: I don't know what I want anymore.

ADONIS: Am I a trigger?

SELENE: No. Maybe. Yes, I think so.

ADONIS: Then, I should go.

SELENE: No, I need you to stay. Research manic depression.

ADONIS: (Reading) It says manic depression is the same as bipolar disorder... Periods of hypersexuality followed by asexuality...

SELENE: (Indifferent)

ADONIS: That's you.

SELENE: I've been trying to tell you.

ADONIS: You need help.

SELENE: You're not hearing me.

ADONIS: (Reading) You need medication.

SELENE: Stop!

ADONIS: Why are we not having sex?

SELENE: Because now I love you.

ADONIS: (Internally) Ha!

SELENE: (Internally) I hate you!

ADONIS: (Internally) What an actress!

SELENE: (Internally) What a jerk!

Aftershocks

Behind the Scenes | Zero, Jess Spink

Here, (packing kitchen knife) kill me.
Never, huh?

The apartment's empty again.
Not even six months!

No worries, though:
Emptiness breeds forgetfulness.

And since you ripped all the pictures
Out of the frames,
No chance of nostalgia.

I talk senselessly,
You remain silent.
If you speak, you will rage!

I won't believe your rage!
You know this. And so,
You don't bother.

I feel cheated a little
Because I want to see you squirm.
But I let it go.

It's not the high road.
It's the easy road.

Not even six months!
Maybe we had sex three times.

That is, you and I, together.
Not counting outside us!

I blamed you for this!
You blamed me for the bugs!

Bugs came in through the windows
When you smoked.

I bought accordion screens
That didn't fit snugly.

You blamed me
For not taking care of you.

I blamed you
For smoke and mirrors.

At its briefest, this is our story.
Blame.

(An opera
Of doused fireworks.)

In this picture, I'm an old goat
Eating everything.

In this one, ripped in half,
I'm a cormorant, back and forth
Between worlds, ravenous.

On the surface,
I made you happy.
Underwater, I devoured you.

Then, I regurgitated you to your other lovers.
That you had other lovers
Made you more beautiful

In my eyes.
They defend you conditionally
So long as you fuck.

They're no different than me
Except they're contemporary.
Current.

In this picture, you're a witch
For Halloween.

I'm a vampire.
Our costumes are minimal.

In our lore, you're a serpent,
Voldemort's Nagini.

I'm a wolf in sheep's skin,
Cesaire, the wolf/father.

You wrap your body around me.
I bite you.

You swallow me whole.
I bite your insides.

You digest me.
I become mush.

I regret
Dying like this,
Inside you.

I didn't want to be a goat,
Or a wolf,
Or pretend to be your father.

I feel the ground rumbling.
Is it the moving truck? No?

It's an earthquake!
Fitting.

A stampede of all the scorned lovers
Swallowed whole by the earth.

My kin.
They're coming to claim me!

I walk out
To meet them,

Empty-handed,
My keys on the kitchen counter.

MATRIX

Bullets | Smash Into Pieces

ADONIS: Holy fucking shit! I dodged a bullet! (Bobs and weaves)

GOD: (Laughing) Ha! You think so?

ADONIS: (Contemplating) Wait. I didn't dodge a bullet. (Puts his hand on chest) I got shot in the heart! (Mimics taking bullets to the chest)

GOD: The walking dead.

ADONIS: It hurts! I'm such an idiot!

GOD: (Nodding)

ADONIS: No, I'm blessed. For what I learned.

GOD: (Frowning) Don't give me that 'blessed' shit.

ADONIS: There is a silver lining though.

GOD: Silver lining, yes.

ADONIS: One, I stopped lying to everyone—and took that power back. No one has power over me now.

GOD: Yes!

ADONIS: Two, I know myself better.

GOD: You're a freak! Even more than I thought.

ADONIS: Three, I made art from it.

GOD: For me, that's number one.

ADONIS: Four, I had a lot of fun. Amazing sex! Great memories...

GOD: Now, lie down and die. That's the only way you're moving on from this.

ADONIS: (Lying down) She's a monster. Because she looks like an angel.

GOD: That's how it works. It's writers, like you, that make them ugly. You let your emotions get in the way. (Sighing) They're beautiful—all my fallen angels!

Five Remembrances (Of Selene)

SAD GIRLZ LUV MONEY Remix | Amaarae, Kali Uchis, Moliy

My nature is to be exploited.
I cannot escape being taken advantage of.
    (I'm a masochist.)

My nature is to be heartbroken.
I cannot escape heartache.
    (I wallow in feelings.)

My nature is to die many figurative deaths.
I cannot escape these deaths.
    (They're too poetic.)

My nature is to love what is unlovable.
I cannot escape my attraction to whoring.
    (I like to role play.)

My lust is my one true characteristic.
I cannot escape the consequences of my lust.
    (Selene romanticized being a whore.
    I romanticized making her my whore.)

I live (and die) in this fantasy (over and over).

    There can be no other ending.

90% Totality (About the Author)

 *For Sure* **Future Islands**

I blossomed for a fake sun.
Or, a false moon.
Still, I blossomed.

There is no other bloom.

SPYING GLASS

Foreshadow | **ENHYPEN**

(Phone call)

SELENE: Good morning daddy.

ADONIS: I had the most intense dream about you last night.

SELENE: Tell me.

ADONIS: I was trying to visit you in the spirit realm. There was a cat with me. I think it was Olivia. We were inside the speaker of a television. There were holes in the walls. I could hear your voice. You were talking to your roommates. I could also hear whatever show was on the television. Then, we were in your apartment, or an apartment that resembled your apartment except the walls were bare. There was no art, no plants, nothing. Way less furniture too, just a couch. I could hear you talking to your roommates somewhere nearby. Then, we were in your stairwell, or a stairwell that resembled your stairwell except there was no ground floor, and no top floor. The stairs went on forever in both directions. There was a lot of clutter in the stairwell, all the stuff you'd find in an attic or basement. Olivia was climbing up the stairs. I followed her. Your voice, your conversation, followed us or led us, I couldn't tell. But you weren't talking to us. We were eavesdropping. I followed Olivia up a flight of stairs. Then my foot got stuck in a hole, or got snagged on something. I couldn't free it. Olivia climbed out of view. I tried to free myself with increasing panic. Then, I glimpsed someone coming up the stairs. I stilled myself as if to hide but there was nowhere to hide. She saw me, your roommate! An acute feeling of shame, and vulnerability overtook me. Suddenly, whatever had hold of my foot pulled me to the ceiling, and I hung upside down as if caught in a snare. Your roommate started laughing. She called to you. I wanted to die. I tried frantically to rouse myself from the dream. My body and brain spasmed. You were coming up the stairs. Then, you saw me! I felt so embarrassed I wanted to die. I painfully forced myself awake, so I didn't have to suffer your gaze anymore. But I felt extreme vertigo, and had to get up to drink a glass of water to settle myself. I still have a lopsided headache.

SELENE: What time was it when you woke up from the dream?

ADONIS: Around 2 am.

SELENE: (Contemplating) You shouldn't spy on me. Not in the spirit realm.

ADONIS: I know. I don't know why I dreamt it.

SELENE: Because even though you say you're not jealous, you are. (Laughing) It's ok.

ADONIS: I love you.

SELENE: I know. (Laughing) I like it.

(Annotated)

INTERLUDES'
PLAYLISTS

Infinity | Infinity Ink

CORONA #2

I Have (Broken the Spell Though)

Lie to Me | Depeche Mode

Do you have a witch in your bed?
Do you have a fer-de-lance in your bed?
Yes indeed I do have a witch in my bed.

Do you have a nude woman smoking a pipe in your bed?
Yes I do have the ashes of her incense in my bed.
Do you have a witch in your bed?

Yes I do have an imprint of a woman lying on the sheets.
Do you have a mahogany coffin in your bed?
Yes indeed I do have a witch in my bed.

Do you have the priestess Medusa's head on a pillow?
Yes I do have her hair-wrapped head in my armpit.
Do you have a witch in your bed?

Yes I do have her tarot cards and crystals in my bed.
Do you have "you're dead to me" in your bed?
Yes indeed I do have a witch in my bed.

What do you have above your headboard?
Do you have a large textile of the moon with two faces?
Do you have a witch in your bed?
Yes indeed I do have a witch in my bed.

(Inception) [Alternate World]

As poet I keep reinventing myself, and my position.

Runaway	Kanye West, Pusha T	9:08
Love-Hate-Sex-Pain	Godsmack	5:15
Careful What You Say	Class Actress	5:12
Holes	Electric Guest	2:46
Ain't No Sunshine	Bill Withers	2:05
A Cosmic Yes	Bearcubs	4:18
Icarus	White Hinterland	3:48
Power & Control	MARINA	3:46
Looking for Love in the Anthropocene	FIELDED	5:01
Svise To Fegari	Dimitris Mitropanos	4:04
VANISH (INTERLUDE).	SUNDERWORLD	1:20
Into the Drama	HTRK	3:51
Untitled 01 / 08.19.2014	Kendrick Lamar	4:08
Sunglasses At Night	Corey Hart	5:21
Walking On A Dream	Empire Of The Sun	3:18
I Dare You	The xx	3:53
Sex God	Samoht	2:18
Holding On	Tirzah	3:20
Achilles Come Down	Gang of Youths	7:02
Flower face – Angela (I dream of you softly)	eevee	1:30
Strip	Little Mix, Sharaya J	3:19
Beyond the Clouds	You'll Never Get to Heaven	4:09
Amandrai	Ali Farka Touré, Ry Cooder	9:24
HAUNTED	Isabel LaRosa	2:18
I'm A Girl You Can Hold IRL	ML Buch	2:39
Everything Was Beautiful	Cruel Youth	2:27
Alternate World (Alternate Age)	**Son Lux**	**4:20**
Loved Ones (Saudades)	Armando Young	5:08
Half Silences	Loma	3:47
Sandpaper Kisses	Martina Topley-Bird	3:52
Mirror	Sigrid	2:36

2h 5m

(Adonis) [Fuck Him All Night]

"Who wants to be just an idea? I want my love to be magic" — Okay Kaya

Wake Up in the Sky	Gucci Mane, Bruno Mars, Kodak Black	3:23
Sex	Ginuwine, Sole	3:50
Say My Name – Luca Lush's Sexy Sax Man Remix	Peking Duk, Benjamin Joseph	4:10
Candyman	Christina Aguilera	3:14
Pretty Boy Swag	Soulja Boy	3:56
Come and Get Your Love – Single Version	Redbone	3:26
Whisked Away Again	Kalaido	4:14
Starlighter	Jupiter	3:15
Sexy M.F.	Prince, The New Power Generation	5:26
Tokyo Love Hotel	Rina Sawayama	4:27
Pygmy Love Song	Francis Bebey	3:51
Toxic – The Voice Performance	Melanie Martinez	3:49
Moby Dick – Intro/Outro Rough Mix	Led Zeppelin	1:38
Closer	Nine Inch Nails	6:13
Habitual Love	Okay Kaya	3:19
Sexy Man	Connan Mockasin	4:06
He Was a Big Freak	Betty Davis	4:08
Water – Remix	Tyla, Travis Scott	3:20
THE RUNNING MAN EXOTIC	Sideshow	1:07
Lover Man	Jimi Hendrix	3:03
Naughty Girl	Qveen Herby	3:09
Sex With Me	Rihanna	3:26
Tell Meeeeee	Salami Rose Joe Louis	0:58
Sick	Donna Missal	3:07
Rasputin	Boney M.	3:41
Lifestyle	Kranium	3:01
Fuck Him All Night	Azealia	2:56
Signs of Love Makin'	Tyrese	4:06
Lovestained	Hope Tala	2:55
Ma Cherie	Naika	3:27
Fantastic Man	William Onyeabor	6:26

1h 55m

(Fog) [100MPH]

"Where do we go? (Sweet child) Where do we go now?" — Guns N' Roses

Opening	Dora Jar	2:43
Sex Paranoia	Goldie Boutilier	4:13
DODGING BULLETS	OSVISS	3:03
Spaceship	Aaron Taylor	3:06
Hysteria	Def Leppard	5:54
Day I Die	DeathbyRomy	2:57
Detroit	Disasterpeace	1:20
Motion	Boy Harsher	3:59
Pursuit	Pixel Grip	3:55
Gasolina	Daddy Yankee	3:12
Somewhere I Belong	Linkin Park	3:33
Fear is your Only God	Mala Sangre	4:26
Droid Rage	OGRE Sound	1:51
Sweet Child O' Mine	Guns N' Roses	5:56
Enough!!	A Tribe Called Quest	3:20
Daddy Issues	The Neighbourhood	4:20
Mount Everest	Labrinth	2:37
Earthquakes and Sharks	Brandtson	2:57
Terr et Tiwa dorment	Alain Goraguer	0:49
Smokescreen	Pearly Drops	2:58
360 Baby	Dizzy Fae	2:28
Play with Fire	Sam Tinnesz, Yacht Money	3:00
Look Closer	Michael A	6:28
Taste – Moon Boots Remix	Rhye, Moon Boots	4:53
Where Are You Now	Lost Frequencies, Calum Scott	2:28
Highway to Hell	AC/DC	3:28
100 Miles An Hour	Labrinth	3:01
California Love – Original Version	2Pac, Roger, Dr. Dre	4:44
Transdimensional	TAAHLIAH, KAVARI	4:49
HEAVEN'S GATES	DEVAULT, Izzy Camina	3:08
Backseat	Eric Saade	3:32

2h 5m

(This) [Life]

Headliners for my death parade. (RIP Tour 2024)

Open My Door	Alice Phoebe Lou	2:33
Sex money feelings die	Lykke Li	2:19
Na Na Na (Na Na Na Na Na Na Na Na Na)	My Chemical Romance	3:25
Purple Haze	Jimi Hendrix	2:50
Heat Waves	Glass Animals	3:58
Cinnamon Girl	Lana Del Rey	5:00
Already Gone	Sleeping At Last	4:03
Don't Say Goodbye	Alok, Ilkay Sencan, Tove Lo	3:06
Escapism.	RAYE, 070 Shake	4:32
Tension (Interlude)	BØRNS	1:34
All You Need	Victoria Monét	3:44
Mercy (2022 Edit)	What So Not, MØ	3:17
Giant Steps – Mono	John Coltrane	4:47
Smooth Operator – Single Version	Sade	4:18
Phantasmagoria in Two	Tim Buckley	3:28
Venus as a Boy	Björk	4:42
Continuum	Tanerélle	3:49
Supersoaker	Eartheater	3:04
A Forest	Clan of Xymox	5:39
How Do I Connect To The Spirits?	vöx	3:25
One Dance	Drake, Wizkid, Kyla	2:53
Run This Town	JAY-Z, Rihanna, Kanye West	4:27
When There Is No Sun	Sun Ra	4:35
Sweet	Cigarettes After Sex	4:51
Feeling Good	Nina Simone	2:54
Running with the Wolves	AURORA	3:14
This Is A Life	Son Lux, Mitski, David Byrne	2:41
Love Drought	Beyoncé	3:57
Happiest Year	Jaymes Young	3:48
Born, Never Asked	Laurie Anderson	4:56
You And Me In Time	Broadcast	1:24

1h 53m

(Ebb & Flow) [Eudaemonia]

Adonis drifting in The Narrows...

Lipstick on the Glass	Wolf Alice	4:08
Sexbomb	Tom Jones, Mousse T.	3:32
0594 Help	Haich Ber Na	3:46
Ebb & Flow	FELIVAND	3:30
All The Highs	San Holo	3:26
Coming Back	James Blake, SZA	3:15
Where's My Love	SYML	3:22
Harvest Moon	Poolside	6:08
Crying on the Subway	Hana Vu	2:44
Lover's Hymn	El-Funoun Palestinian Popular Dane Troupe	5:44
Four	The Wrecks	2:38
Weight of Love	The Black Keys	6:50
Tulip	Jesca Hoop	5:07
I'm Still in Love with You	Sean Paul, Selene, Jeremy Harding, Murray Elias	4:33
Give It To Me	Miya Folick	5:10
All I Want	Kodaline	5:05
Just like Heaven	The Cure	3:32
Dissolving	Hannah Cohen	3:37
Everything Belongs To You	Joesef	1:51
Mask	Niykee Heaton	2:59
I Miss You	Alexis Munroe	2:37
Hearing Damage	Thom Yorke	5:03
Moon Undah Water	Puma Blue	5:32
New Normal	Selene Alex Sloan	3:07
Emotional Machine	MARINA	3:15
Favorite Crime	Olivia Rodrigo	2:32
Eudaemonia	Them Are Us Too	4:21
Sidetracked / Perfect Lover	Tanerélle	4:02
Tears In The Typing Pool	Broadcast	2:12
I'm Still Wearing His Jacket	Molly Nilsson	4:05
Glow	Alice Phoebe Lou	2:45

2h

(The End) [Die 4 You]

Dying, Adonis inhabited Selene. She felt this as a maturation, her own little death.

The End (Of a Dream – Shlohmo Cover	tomemitsu	5:12
Senegal Seduction	Charlotte Adigéry	5:06
.- . . . - . . _ _-.- - -	. . - . - .. . . . - ..	7:18
A Little Death	The Neighbourhood	3:29
Sunlight	Hozier	4:17
Please don't go	eevee	4:19
This Insatiable Love	Kid Francescoli, Julia Minkin	4:02
Misery Is a Butterfly	Blonde Redhead	5:07
Call It Fate, Call It Karma	Moon Panda	4:00
Éternité	Hante.	4:17
Monk's Robes	Deradoorian	4:46
Narratives	Breakup Shoes	3:06
Tonight I Feel Like Kafka	Jealous of the Birds	3:09
Bending Light	Beacon	2:52
1965	Zella Day	3:38
No One Else	Tanerélle, barnacle boi	3:12
Shake well before use	YSI	5:40
Enemy	Imagine Dragons, JID, Arcane, League of Legends	2:53
Whirl pool	Yoshinori Sunahara	6:28
As I Opened the Window	Kenneth Patchen	3:56
She's in Parties	Bauhaus	5:46
Hotter Than Your Instincts	Khushi	3:37
Heaven	I Monster	3:57
The Moon and the Sky	Sade	4:28
Marked for Death	Emma Ruth Rundle	3:40
Vampires Will Never Hurt You	My Chemical Romance	5:27
Die 4 You	Perfume Genius	3:33
Loving, Loving	Vera Sola	3:20
That's Not My Real Life	Cherry Glazer, Delicate Steve	2:57
The Apocalypse Song	St. Vincent	3:47
Suddenly I Know Who You Are	Jadu Heart	3:02

2h 10m

(Fog) [Reprise]

"I could have sworn I saw a light coming on" — Radiohead

Foggy Morning	Golden Gemini	1:58
Xenogenesis	TheFatRat	3:53
Self Assembly	Ochre	2:18
Quintessence	Coleman Hawkins Quartet	4:45
Fantas for Electric Guitar	Caterina Barbieri, Walter Zanetti	7:30
The Last Ray - Remastered	This Mortal Coil	3:35
Adonis	Etro Anime	4:55
The King's Tulips	David Motion, Sally Potter	3:02
Portofino 2	Raymond Scott	2:15
Tunan	Mamman Sani	3:22
Once Upon a Dream	Invadable Harmony	1:00
A Glass Ceiling	Sin Fang	1:30
MPH	MIKNNA	3:33
*Firecracker*ファイアークラッカー	YELLOW MAGIC ORCHESTRA	4:52
Bond At The Border - Interlude	Jimmy Whoo	1:23
Saudade	Thievery Corporation	2:09
The Monkey on Your Back	Standing On the Corner	1:21
The Water Rises	Kronos Quartet, Laurie Anderson	2:43
Lost It To Trying	Son Lux	4:43
Sing You Sinners	Fletcher Henderson	2:39
Whiskey Wah	Frank Zappa	1:35
Astral Projection	El Jazzy Chavo	2:34
I Might Be Wrong	Radiohead	4:54
The Electrical Life of Louis Wain	Arthur Sharpe	2:57
Above The Euromechopolis	OGRE Sound	2:10
Atomic Shogun	OGRE Sound	1:37
Promise (Reprise)	Akira Yamaoka	1:45
Love Lasso	Turnstile	1:49
Trois Gymnopedies (First Movement)	Gary Numan	2:44
The Fly	RŮDE	2:02
The Girl Next Door	Tomppabeats	0:51

1h 28m

(Tadow) [Body]

Selene rising out of Adonis' fiction, strutting her stuff (post-Quindecim).

Angel Numbers / Ten Toes	Chris Brown	5:07
Rich Baby Daddy	Drake, Sexyy Red, SZA	5:19
You	Lola Brooke, Bryson Tiller	2:41
Shining	DJ Khaled, Beyoncé, Jay-Z	4:44
Pretty Girls Walk	Big Boss Vette	2:20
Like This	Kelly Rowland, Eve	3:36
Shine on me – Instrumental	Small b	4:58
Not One Thing	Patrice Roberts	3:13
Better Thangs	Ciara, Summer Walker	3:34
Soweto	Victony, Tempoe	2:28
Masterpiece (Mona Lisa)	Jazmine Sullivan	4:06
CUFF IT – WETTER REMIX	Beyoncé	4:09
Snooze – Instrumental	SZA	3:22
How We Roll	Ciara, Chris Brown	3:20
I CAN	Loïc Reyel	3:35
Addicted	Popcaan	2:58
ROCK THE ESSENCE (MASHUP)	Ombre2Choc Remix	4:12
God's Plan	Drake	3:19
Peru – Instrumental	Archie Blackie	3:07
I'm a mess	Omah Lay	2:34
Goddess	D'yani, One Army Ent	3:04
Girl on Fire	Alicia Keys	3:45
I Got You – Instrumental	justonemarcus	3:13
Good Energy	Yung Wylin'	3:12
Tadow	Masego, FKJ	5:01
Everybody	Nicki Minaj, Lil Uzi Vert	3:01
Touch My Body	Mariah Carey	3:25
She Wanna Make Love in the Water	Young Pharaoh	3:32
Lights, Camera, Action!	Mr. Cheeks	4:21
Vibrate Higher	Londrelle, Lalah Delia	5:04
Vulnerable	Yo Trane	3:00

1h 53m

(Verrazano) [1000]

Adonis falling...

Carnival Song/Hi Lily Hi Lo	Tim Buckley	8:50
Volver, volver	Buika	4:21
Dear Prudence	The Beatles	3:55
Madness of the Moon	W & Whale	3:18
Luv(sic.) pt3	Nujabes, Shing02	5:36
You Got to Feed the Fire	Ann Peebles	2:22
Posthumous Forgiveness	Tame Impala	6:06
Jacuzzi Rollercoaster	Róisín Murphy, Ali Love	6:47
Duse Henny	Alia Kadir	2:56
3/12/1998	Lena Platonos	3:35
Already Dead	Juice WRLD	3:51
Space Song	Beach House	5:20
Sisyphus	Andrew Bird	4:07
Chlorine	Twenty One Pilots	5:24
Love Me Like You Hate Me	Rainsford	4:23
• I WON'T DIE •	Tom The Mail Man	2:03
Stroke	BANKS	3:26
Can You Feel My Heart	Bring Me The Horizon	3:48
Deep End	Fousheé	2:21
Love & Hate	Michael Kiwanuka	7:07
I See U	One True God	3:09
Skyline, be mine	Shura	5:16
Virginia Woolf Underwater	Chelsea Wolfe	4:22
Venus	Theatre of Tragedy	5:33
Feel It	Michele Morrone	2:39
Heat	L.A. Rose	3:10
I want to sleep for 1000 years	EKKSTACY	2:15
I Felt Love	Blue Hawaii	3:12
Currents	Drake	2:37
One Evening	Feist	3:36
I'm Tied, To You	Two People	7:12

2h 12m

(Airbnb) [Spring '23]

Cuddling, they hid from shame. Not their own, but their interpretation of the other's. Adonis mused: she likes to be thrown around because she's numbed herself to the world. She can't feel a soft touch. Selene mused: he likes to burrow in my asshole because he sees cleanliness as a lie. He can't get aroused unless it's filth, foul, or forbidden.

Until Morning	James Vickery	3:16
Euphoria	Harper Finn	2:57
All My Love	KIRBY	3:28
Babygirl	Alex Sloane	3:17
Love Is Complicated (The Angels Sing)	Labrinth	3:19
Be With You – Outwild Remix	Rootkit, Outwild, Gloria Kim	4:14
There Is No Greater Love – Live at Philharmonic Hall, NY, NY – February 1964	Miles Davis	10:06
As One	What So Not, Herizen	3:58
Call On Me (with Tove Lo)	SG Lewis, Tove Lo	3:16
Cherry Blossom Ending	Busker Busker	4:20
This Is for the Lover in You	Shalamar	5:04
I Feel Love	Sam Smith	4:14
Eternal Youth	RÜDE	3:25
Trip	Ella Mai	3:33
The Perfect Girl	Mareux	3:14
The First Time Ever I Saw Your Face	Roberta Flack	4:20
When You Watch Me	Poppy Ajudha	3:53
NFWMB	Hozier	4:19
The Spring	Sleep At Last	2:15
I'd Have You Anytime	George Harrison	2:57
In The Dark	DEV	3:46
Get Me High	Anna Thompson, Jake Crocker	2:47
Moments in Love	The Art Of Noise	10:15
The Power Of Love	Frankie Goes To Hollywood	5:32
The Archer	Alexandra Savior	2:25
Addict	Don Louis	2:46
Spring Is Coming With a Strawberry in the Mouth	**Roger Doyle**	**4:23**
DO 4 LOVE	Snoh Aalegra	3:09
Indigo	Alice Gray	3:30
See You In My Dreams	Kat Leon, NOCTURN	3:34
I Need Your Body	Brooke Bentham	4:10

2h 5m

(Four Ethers) [Kaleidoscope]

Seeing, Selene saw herself for the first time through her own eyes. Not through the eyes of her biological mother—whose gaze she yearned for, and died for many times over! Not through the eyes of her adopted parents—judging, condemning. Not through the eyes of her sugar daddies—lusting, plowing. Not through the eyes of Adonis—projecting an innocence that didn't exist.

Four Ethers	serpentwithfeet	4:29
Four Women	Nina Simone	4:24
Swing	Dawn Golden	5:35
Beyond the Clouds	You'll Never Get to Heaven	4:08
Interfaith	Public Memory	3:46
Devil Gaze	Joshual	3:30
Fear of the Water	SYML	4:05
Burning Bridges	Chromatics	1:54
Nont For Sale	Sudan Archives	3:39
Clipped Wings – Secret Circuit Remix	Dengue Fever	4:30
Eternity With You	Adventure Time, Michaela Dietz, Zuzu	2:22
Fallen Star	The Neighbourhood	3:44
Faerie Court (Under Moon)	CLANN	6:52
These Dreams	Heart	4:14
Embody Me	Novo Amor	3:10
Sugar	Zubi, anatu	3:25
Cream – Without Rap Monologue	Prince	4:13
Channel Swimmer	10cc	2:48
Dream Sweet in Sea Major	Miracle Musical	7:00
Mitosis	Eartheater	2:27
Grace	breathe.	3:15
Aurora	K-391, RØRY	2:44
When Under Ether	PJ Harvey	2:22
I Feel Like Breaking up Somebody's Home Tonight	Ann Peebles	2:30
Thanatos	Soap&Skin	2:34
Night-Time Intermission	Charlotte Gainsbourg	2:43
Kaleidoscope	**Flower Face**	**3:08**
True Love	Kanye West, XXXTentacion	2:28
Four	Sleeping At Last	4:51
Call It Fear	Joy Harjo	2:02
Reflection of Youth	EERA	3:44

1h 52m

(Cormorant) [Underwater]

"Down into the depths with fading light" — Bearcubs

All We Ever Wanted Was Everything	Bauhaus	3:52
Apocalypse	Cigarettes After Sex	4:50
2y & 6m	Cindy	4:03
Swimmer	Helena Deland	3:33
Haunted Water	SPELLLING	4:46
How Soon Is Now?	The Smiths	6:48
It's Time For You To Stop Being a Ghost	Sindri Már, Sigfússon, Sin Fang	1:52
Pretty Please	Dua Lipa	3:15
Bullet Proof Soul	Sade	5:25
Peligrosa	Urias	2:29
Sorry About the Carpet	Agar Agar	6:08
Pay Your Way In Pain	St. Vincent	3:04
Shimmer and Disappear	Pram	3:15
13 Beaches	Lana Del Rey	4:56
Life as One	Skinshape	4:18
Liar	Megadeath	3:21
WORTH NOTHING	TWISTED, Oliver Tree	2:45
Sharks	Morphine	2:23
Surf or Not	Connan Mockasin, Andrew VanWyngarden	1:13
Real Headfuck	HTRK	3:25
A Little Wicked	Valerie Broussard	3:30
New Fiction	Little Dragon	4:20
Matrix	Dizzy Gillespie	4:01
Some Heavy Ocean	Emma Ruth Rundle	1:42
You're Not Good Enough	Blood Orange	4:21
Addiction	Kanye West	4:27
Underwaterfall	**Bearcubs**	**4:20**
Feral Love	Chelsea Wolfe	3:22
I'm Not Okay (I Promise)	My Chemical Romance	3:06
The Way It Goes	Sneaks	2:49
No Way Out	Clan of Xymox	4:19

1h 55m

(Goodbye) [Spirited Away]

"I fall but still I try to not lose my way" — Ben Böhmer, Malou

And A Colored Sky Colored Grey	Vincent Gallo	2:03
Saudade	Thievery Corporation	2:09
Danube Incident	Lalo Schifrin	1:58
Four	Miles Davis Quintet	7:13
Furious Angels – Instrumental	Rob Dougan	5:30
Anaphora	Ochre	4:26
Bora Bora Flowers	Jimmy Whoo	1:47
Afghan Dance	Solid Space	1:50
Part Two	Leo Kottke	1:43
Munaye (My Muna)	Mulatu Astatke	5:03
Orford Sentinel	Ochre	1:12
Saying Goodbye	Bruce Dessner, Aaron Dessner, et al	1:45
Angel Falls	Tomas Skyldeberg	5:21
1974	Sleepdealer	1:08
Boardwalk Dulce	Emancipator, Asher Fulero, Dab Records	1:38
Adonis	hubris.	9:17
Cosmic Bloom	Dumbo Gets Mad	1:06
Oceans Apart	Ben Crosland	1:18
04317introduktion	Flughand	2:50
TRISTAN	SebastiAn	2:56
Nudists	Valium Aggelein	1:32
Firecracker	Martin Denny	2:30
Lost In Mind	Ben Böhmer, Malou	3:31
Bewitched	Invadable Harmony	1:09
Intro	The xx	2:08
Midnight Stinger	A Space Love Adventure, Highway Superstar	3:21
Reprise (From "Spirited Away") [Piano Version]	**Nikolai Tal**	**1:39**
Ballad For Space Lovers	Space	2:19
Blades of the Goddess (Titles)	OGRE Sound	1:36
Accadde a Bali	Arawak	2:27
Eye To Eye	David Motion, Sally Potter	3:32

1h 27m

(Disquiet) [Coming Down]

"Am I underground or am I in-between? Am I still alive or has the light gone black" — Phantogram

Apply	Glasser	4:59
Did We Live Too Fast?	Got A Girl	3:50
No Moon At All	Julie London	1:54
The World (Is Going Up in Flames)	Charles Bradley, Menahan Street Band	3:22
If I Was Vox	Drew Milligan, John Moabi, Gary Forbes	4:26
Some Type Of Skin	AURORA	3:13
Holes in Your Coffin	PHILDEL	4:08
Love Is to Die	Warpaint	4:52
Hush	The Marias	3:02
Kif	Dimitris Mitropanos	3:16
When I'm Small	Phantogram	4:09
Day 7.5093	Nilüfer Yanya	3:42
Waterlily	Deradoorian	2:06
Lebanese Blonde	Thievery Corporation	4:49
Rip out the Wings of a Butterfly	YULLOLA	1:53
Don't Fall In Love	Still Corners	3:54
Black Metal	Helena Deland	3:42
Swim	Jack's Mannequin	4:16
Flame on Flame (a Slow Dirge)	Kishi Bashi	4:46
P. 11-12 May 19	Kenneth Patchen	0:52
Dance to You	Morly	4:04
Beginning to Blue	Still Corners	3:12
Poem of Dead Song	Broadcast	2:32
Sunsetz	Cigarettes After Sex	3:35
Like the Moon	Future Islands	4:40
All Your Yeahs	Beach House	3:48
Coming Down	Dum Dum Girls	6:29
L Is For Love	El Perro del Mar	4:33
Journal of Ardency	Class Actress	3:45
Phoenix	Martina Topley-Bird	2:45
Are You Filming Me?	twst	3:08

1h 53m

(Photograph) [My Own]

"The truth will set you free. But first, it'll piss you off (hey)" — N.E.R.D.

I've Shaken Up	vōx, Salyu	3:07
New Person, Same Old Mistakes	Tame Impala	6:03
Lemon	N.E.R.D, Rihanna, Pharrell Williams	3:40
Pay My Debts	Beacon	2:58
Radio	Lana Del Rey	3:35
Feels Right	Crystal Skies, RUNN	3:33
In Another Life	Son Lux	2:24
Set it on Fire	Blood Cultures	3:33
To Perth, before the border closes	Julia Jacklin	2:57
Questioning My Mind	Ambar Lucid	4:15
Emptiness	One True God, Roniit	2:30
Lost in Echoes	Caskets	3:38
Cosmic Bloom	Dumbo Gets Mad	1:06
Photograph	Def Leppard	4:08
If We're Being Honest	Novo Amor	3:55
Prototype / Limit to Your Love	WOOM	4:39
NEW MAGIC WAND	Tyler, The Creator	3:15
Sugar Water	Flower Face	3:19
Metallic Taste of Patience	Eartheater	3:50
Mind Body Problem	Dorian Electra	3:46
Search & Rescue	Drake	4:32
Late Night Feelings	Mark Ronson, Lykke Li	4:11
Don't Break The Silence – Instrumental	070 Shake	1:55
Chance	Angel Olsen	5:59
NO SURPRISE	Turnstile	0:45
LONELY DEZIRES	Turnstile, Blood Orange	2:43
Taking My Own Advice	Baird	3:13
Lack of Love	Adonis, Charles B.	4:28
Meta Angel	FKA twigs	4:19
Red Room	Hiatus Kaiyote	3:52
Key 手掛かり	YELLOW MAGIC ORCHESTRA	4:36

1h 50m

(Adonis) [Emotional Masochist]

"To believe a lie is the only crime" — Glass Candy

Once-Upon-A-Time	Jamilah Barry	2:44
Flowers	Troi Irons	2:58
U turn me on (but u give me depression)	LØLØ	2:27
Tongue	Maribou State, Holly Walker	5:04
Witch in the Cut	Milo Korbenski	3:15
Tell It to My Heart	Paris Paloma	2:53
Not Time Yet	Jay-Jay Johanson	4:58
Keep It Going	dvsn	3:53
Let Me Down	Quinn XCII, Chlesea Cutler	2:29
Pourquoi tu me fous plus des coups?	An Luu	4:40
Baby Pillz	Dizzy Fae	2:27
Did It Hurt?	Ellise	2:44
We Will Become Silhouettes	The Postal Service	5:00
Somebody That I Used To Know	Gotye, Kimbra	4:04
I'm Not Asking	Odina	2:50
SPIT IN MY FACE!	ThxSoMch	2:27
Skin Tight	Ravyn Lenae, Steve Lacy	3:47
Circling	Eyas	3:24
Make daddy proud	blackbear	3:28
YOU AGAINST YOURSELF	Ruel	2:26
Dream Girl Evil	Florence + The Machine	3:47
Burning Pile	Mother Mother	4:22
Good Looking	Suki Waterhouse	3:34
Crystalline	The Midnight	6:02
HEAD	Devon Again	1:51
BLOODY FUTURE	Kilo Kish	3:25
EMOTIONAL MASOCHIST	**Kent Osborne**	**2:09**
Kosmic Luv	Dizzy Fae	2:18
Go As a Dream	Caroline Polachek	3:27
I Cannot Sleep at Night	K.I.D	2:51
Damaged Goods	La Roux, Gang of Four	3:54

1h 45m

(Klartraum) [4U]

Fucking, they involuntarily revealed their secrets. Not in words—in how they came, what got them off.

Because	Elliott Smith	2:19
Spin Me Around	The Marías	2:26
Body	MoonLander, SoMo	2:30
Go Down on You	The Memories	1:00
Taste of Your Love	Mochi	2:08
Little Wing	Jimi Hendrix	2:25
Birth To Death In Slow Motion	Valium Aggelein	1:23
Klartraum	Gurr	2:06
Santorini Coffee	melvitto	2:14
Pligose me	Panos Marinos	2:30
What You Know Bout Love	Pop Smoke	2:40
ANTIGRAVITY	KUNZITE, Lee Perry, Ratatat	1:53
Sophia's Theme (Reprise)	Danny Elfman	2:32
Elastic	Joey Purp	2:06
There Is No Greater Love – Live in Los Angeles, 1954	Dinah Washington, Clifford Brown	2:15
Do You Want a Man – Heaven & Hell Remix	William Onyeabor, The Vaccines, et al	2:25
Big Ten Inch Record	Aerosmith	2:15
Crawled Out Of The Sea (Interlude)	Laura Marling	1:16
Loved Back to Life	Andy Hull and Robert McDowell	0:29
Rasga	Urias, Maffalda	2:32
Treat Me	Chlöe	2:29
Elon Musk	Indika Sam	2:30
Eruption	Van Halen	1:42
You Really Got Me	Van Halen	2:36
Kool Aid	KIRBY	2:33
For You	Kadhja Bonet	2:39
4U	Ojerime	2:16
LOVE	Jhené Aiko	2:36
Recipe!	Jean Deaux	2:29
99 Pounds	Ann Peebles	2:18
STRUT	EMELINE	1:57

1h 7m

(Motel Vacancy) [Death Fantasy]

They move to Curaçao. They open a hotel on the beach. They live happily ever after... Until Adonis is eaten by sharks!

Amateur Night	Dream, Ivory	2:26
We Might Even Be Falling In Love (Interlude)	Victoria Monét	0:51
Makeitliveforever	Knxwledge	1:50
Vacation	drea the vibe dealer, Blake Davis	2:28
Multiply	Dora Jar	2:16
Thru My Hair	¿Téo?	1:40
It's like you're right there	aimless	1:34
Running Away (Time)	VANO 3000, BADBADNOTGOOD, Samuel T. Herring	1:32
Caught Up	Dee Gatti	2:10
Moi je joue	Brigitte Bardot	1:42
My Body	Perfume Genius	2:17
Note To Self	Jim-E Stack, Empress Of	2:17
Blue	Madi Sipes & The Painted Blue	2:17
Enjoy the silence	Fousheé	2:27
Chapel Of Love	Jimmy Whoo	1:39
Killer lover boy	SEB	2:14
Da Rockwilder	Method Man, Redman	2:16
LIMB	Planet Giza	1:44
Sickly Suite Part Three: Gone	I Monster	0:57
No Face	Haley Heynderickx	1:56
Smoking at Midnight	Tomppabeats	1:35
Ambulance	Bnny	2:01
Smile #2	Slauson Malone 1, Maxo	1:17
After the Beep	Tanerélle	2:21
Summers Over Interlude	Drake, Majid Jordan	1:46
The Hunter Gets Captured By The Game – Lofi Flip	uChill, The Marvelettes, LOUALLDAY	2:07
DEATH FANTASY	Kilo Kish, Miguel	2:09
Love In The Future (Intro)	John Legend	0:40
Goji Berry Sunset	Jealous of the Birds	2:17
Cumulous Potion (For the Clouds to Sing)	Salami Rose Joe Louis	2:27
Morning	Amaria	2:28

59m

(Mist) [Shape of Things]

They lie in bed unable to sleep. Ghosts (other lovers) skim the ceiling. They don't name them.
They wish them away. Adonis yearns for morning, Selene for dreamless sleep.

Quintessence	Quincy Jones	4:22
Rough Sex	Moon Hooch	4:14
Lunes 1 De Abril	The Holydrug Couple	1:15
あまい囁き *Sweet whispers*	Sekitō Shigeo	3:27
M i s t	eevee	1:58
French inhale	[bsd.u]	1:48
Warm Dream	Weeze, Carli & The Dark	5:08
Le perv	Carpenter Brut	4:16
Blue Train – Alternate Take	John Coltrane	9:58
Maya	Ahmed Malek	2:36
Can't Leave the Night	BADBADNOTGOOD	4:40
Insert (The Fall)	Mononome	1:24
Turn Gold to Sand	Ásgeir	4:07
Battle Without Honor Or Humanity	HOTEI	2:28
Opening Night	Jessica Pratt	1:39
I Want To Talk About You	Ryo Fukui	6:32
Dance Of The Persian Serpent	Little Steven, The Interstellar Jazz Renegades	1:48
Our Hearts Condemn Us	Jozef Van Wissem	5:26
Now You're Moving	Drug Store Romeos	2:37
Slow Gemini	Abyss Sounds	2:10
STRIP TEASE SYMPHONY	Jimmy Whoo, Rose	2:17
Sound of Violence – Demo	Other Lives	1:49
Dream Fortress	Grimes	5:00
It's Time For You To Stop Being a Ghost	Sindri Már Sigfússon, Sin Fang	1:51
Pentagram	Gui Boratto	3:06
Vampires	Bat For Lashes	3:02
Shape of Things to Come	Paul Keogh	3:01
When First I Love	Martin Denny	2:24
Epistrophy – Alternate Take	Thelonious Monk, John Coltrane	3:10
The Kiss	Bryce Dessner, Aaron Dessner, et al	1:37
I Don't Want You To Go	Dario Marianelli	4:58

1h 44m

(Selene) [False Moon]

"To tell a lie is the only crime" — Glass Candy

Velvet Green	Tsar B	4:12
WHY AREN'T WE HAVING SEX?	Liza Owen	3:32
Gospel For A New Century	Yves Tumor	3:18
Lucid Dreams	Juice WRLD	3:59
Welcome	Bôa	5:05
Take Care of Yourself	Le Siren	3:11
IF I Could Hold Your Soul	Cities Aviv	1:47
The Beat's Alive	Glass Candy	5:38
SOMEONE ELSE'S PROBLEM	Ruel	2:40
Fue mejor	Kali Uchis, SZA	3:50
In the Night	Deb Never	3:17
Falling from the Sky	Kailee Morgue, KiNG MALA	2:44
Necessary Death	Rotana	2:44
Purple Rain – 2015 Paisley Park Remaster	Prince	8:44
Paramount Tether	Febueder	4:14
Woo x I was never there (sped up)	accelerate, creamy, 11:11 Music Group	2:58
Deranged for Rock & Roll	Chelsea Wolfe	3:31
I Feel Like I'm Drowning	Two Feet	3:05
Love Bomb	AVII KNIGHT	3:16
Ever fallen?	Kate Peytavin	2:48
SIREN	Shygirl	3:56
Fire for You	Cannons	3:51
There's No Tomorrow	Clan of Xymox	7:09`
Now Awake	Jelly Crystal	4:38
Savior	St. Vincent	3:26
Masochism	Ky Vöss	3:25
False Moon	Them Are Us Too	5:52
Love/Paranoia	Tame Impala	3:05
Bittersweet	Lianne La Havas	4:52
Golden Light	STRFKR	4:43
Afterglow	Luna Li	3:18

2h 3m

(Quintessence) [Kaleidoscope]

Drifting, they were doomed. Doomed to haunt each other in every other relationship.

Quintessence	aspidistrafly	4:22
BLOOM IN PARIS	_BY.ALEXANDER, Charles Bukowski	5:08
Believer	Imagine Dragons	3:24
Stay Open	Cecile Believe	2:23
Wind	Akeboshi	3:40
Tokyo Drifting	Glass Animals, Denzel Curry	3:36
Mussel Bay (Outro)	Sad Night Dynamite	2:49
Meet You in the Dark	Das Kope	2:55
Red Morning	Devics	4:42
Sukoon	Hassan & Roshaan, Shae Gill	4:15
Blue Orange Green	Jimmy Whoo, Chilly Gonzalez	3:18
Feels Like We Only Go Backwards	Tame Impala	3:12
The Faerie Court (Under Sun)	CLANN	4:14
The Wind Cries Mary	Jimi Hendrix	3:20
Tie That Binds	Drake	5:36
Everglade	Collard	2:57
Emo Girl	Machine Gun Kelly, WILLOW	2:39
Moths in the Darkness	Meltt	3:47
Luna (Moon of Claiming)	Cemeteries	6:00
Laugh Clown	Xenia Rubinos	4:04
On My Own	Darci	2:51
Sign Of The Wolf	Pentagram	3:10
Dust	Pan Daijing	3:59
B-Side	Khruangbin, Leon Bridges	4:34
Feeling Dizzy	Everything But The Girl	4:14
High Alone	Sevdaliza	3:53
Kaleidoscope	**Champagne Drip, Crystalline**	**3:31**
Sing about love	Fousheé	3:34
Haze	breathe.	3:47
Closer to Grey	Chromatics	2:44
Within You, Within Me	Meltt	3:18

1h 56m

(Space) [Take Me]

"So you wanna be alien too, huh?" — Rexy

Stargazing	The Neighbourhood	3:37
Star	Machinedrum, Mono/Poly, Tanerélle	3:42
Dear Darkness – Demo	PJ Harvey	3:09
My Name Is Human	Highly Suspect	4:19
A Sky Full of Stars	Coldplay	4:28
Starboy	The Weeknd, Daft Punk	3:50
Blues for an Astronaut	El Jazzy Chavo	2:20
Space Ghost Coast To Coast	Glass Animals	3:07
Space Truckin'	Deep Purple	4:34
Effeminacy	Sega Bodega	2:56
Alien	Rexy	4:22
Borderlines and Aliens	GROUPLOVE	3:50
UFO	ESG	2:58
STAR WALKIN' (League of Legends Worlds Anthem)	Lil Nas X	3:31
Constellations	Jade LeMac	3:20
My Moon My Man	Feist, Boys Noize	6:41
Stars Align	Majid Jordan, Drake	4:21
Jumpsuit	Twenty One Pilots	3:59
Cocktails in Space	Nmesh	3:21
I Thought I Was An Alien	Soko	2:19
Space Girl	Frances Forever	3:51
All The Stars	Kendrick Lamar, SZA	3:52
The Dark Side	Kronos Quartet, Laurie Anderson	1:11
Afterlife	Madisenxoxo	2:34
God Is a Circle	Yves Tumor	3:33
New Gods	Grimes	3:16
Take Me to the Sun	ELSZ	5:14
Spacey Love	Apollo Bebop	3:07
Heaven in Your Head	Nuclear Daisies	3:14
Don't Delete The Kisses	Wolf Alice	4:34
Soft Universe	AURORA	4:00

1h 53m

(Rebirth) [Overture]

"Wake up to your girl. For now, let's call her, Cleopatra, Cleopatra" — Frank Ocean

Begin Again	Ben Böhmer	2:42
Night Rise	System Olympia	7:19
Spindrift	Colin Stetson	6:28
I X Love – Long Version	Charles Mingus	7:41
Atlantic Postcard	The Holydrug Couple	3:06
Last Night Over Norway	Funki Porcini	1:38
Pyramids	Frank Ocean	9:53
Devil's Dance	Cortex	2:29
Sunrise	Coldplay	2:31
Chorégraphie du départ	Daprinski	1:24
Spring Rounds from Rite of Spring	Alice Coltrane	6:02
Indra	Thievery Corporation	5:23
Nothing Else Matters	Metallica	6:29
Simbo	Ali Farka Touré, Toumani Diabaté	3:59
Pas De Deux	Evgueni Galperine, Sacha Galperine	1:58
Adonis	LBLVNC	3:48
Mannequin Metric	Cavern of Anti-Matter	4:15
360°	BFRND	3:44
Wake Up	Rage Against The Machine	6:04
Big Fun Never Ending Nightmare [75 BPM]	Vegyn	2:02
Peepshow	Pram	3:29
Space Is the Place	Men I Trust	3:12
Donnie Darko	Let's Eat Grandma	11:19
Trailing Memory	Son Lux	1:57
Post Tropical Cyclone	Yuuki Matthews	2:37
Déshominisation (I)	Alain Goraguer	3:50
Overture	Momoko Kikuchi	2:23
Beyond Love	Deep Koliis	5:17
My Isle Of Golden Dreams	Martin Denny	2:20
Cool Green World	Barry Adamson	3:32
Awake	Tycho	4:44

2h 13m

(Dream of Clarity) [Baby]

Loving, they were incompatible. Adonis wanted a sex doll. Selene wanted a father (not a daddy).

That's Us	Drellas Dream Drops	8:03
Sex In Public	Menna	2:23
Ode to a Conversation Stuck in Your Throat	Del Water Gap	3:19
So Into You	Atlanta Rhythm Section	4:20
A Little Place Called The Moon	AURORA	4:10
High You Are (Branchez Remix)	What So Not, Branchez	3:33
No-One in the World	Locust	6:41
I'm on Top	Otha	3:22
Up All Night	The War On Drugs	6:23
Ikimiz Bir Fidaniz	Kamuran Akkor	3:30
A Different Kind of Love	Son Lux	3:38
Alive	What So Not	0:50
Gemini (Ekali Remix)	What So Not, Ekali	4:01
Every Night	Josef Salvat	3:43
Be My Husband	Nina Simone	3:20
Fall in Love with You.	Montell Fish	2:12
Breakfast in Bed	Rayana Jay	1:56
Desire Lines	Deerhunter	6:44
Time for Us	Nicolas Jaar	7:40
I Like That	Janelle Monáe	3:20
Diamondz	Phleaux	3:09
Outer Space	Joey Gx	3:33
Where or When	Onyx Collective, Kelsey Lu	3:10
Loved by You	KIRBY	4:16
I Know Places	Lykke Li	6:26
Riders on the Storm	The Doors	7:14
Dream Baby Dream	**Suicide**	**6:24**
Love	Erykah Badu	6:01
Let The Lights On	Sorry	3:03
A Little God In My Hands	Swans	7:08
In the Mirror	Lena Raine	9:37

2h 23m

(Spoken Word) [Heart Stop]

"Lover forgive me my guilt is my only crime" — She Wants Revenge

Green Gold Grey	Shuta Hasunuma, U-zhaan, Arto Lindsay	4:41
Sex X Money X Sneakers	BJ The Chicago Kid	3:32
Dirtytalk	Sebastian Mikael, Najee Janey	4:22
Blessings	Chance the Rapper, Ty Dolla $ign, et al	3:50
Monologue	She Wants Revenge	4:54
Energy	Sampa the Great, Nadeem Din-Gabisi	4:59
Fullmoon	Ryuichi Sakamoto	5:13
Bussifame	Dawn Richard	4:33
Muscle	Easter	3:42
Secrecy Is Incredibly Important To The Both of Them	Yves Tumor	3:53
Solo (Reprise)	Frank Ocean	1:19
Already Falling	Puma Blue	4:16
Axolotl	The Veils	3:03
Lost Ones	Ms. Lauryn Hill	5:34
No War Bride	Algebra Suicide	1:26
Replaceable Heads	Soko	4:42
LICK IT N SPLIT	Zebra Katz, Shygirl	3:00
Other Men's Girls	Baxter Dury	3:45
Love Attack	Fhin	3:01
See How	Young Fathers	2:01
Badlands	Mia Carucci	2:55
Rise	Zamilska	3:58
Intro/Spectrum	HÆLOS	1:31
Beauty	LOVE SUPREME	3:59
Reprise – Live	Erykah Badu	2:15
Dark Dopamine Ceremony	Class Actress, Madeaux	2:31
Heart Stop	Wax Tailor, Jennifer Charles	2:55
If Loving You is Wrong	Against All Logic	3:56
Too Many Voices	Andy Stott	6:07
You, at the End	Lafawndah	4:12
Touch U (Find a Way Pt. 2)	YULLOLA	1:53

1h 51m

(The Ether) [Other Side]

"I sway in place to a slow disco" — St. Vincent

Windowpane	Mild High Club	3:57
Disco	Sextile	3:30
Tell Your New Lovers	Sin Fang, Sóley, Örvar Smárason	6:21
Monolithic	Cults	3:39
Parenthesis	Tricky, The Antlers	2:57
Half Hour Verve	Harvey Causon	4:05
Cover Me Slowly	Deerhunter	1:22
Fast Slow Disco	St. Vincent	3:17
Dealer	Lana Del Rey	4:34
Naturopathe	Sega Bodega, Charlotte Gainsbourg	3:16
Where Is The Sun???	Blue Hawaii	2:53
The World Retreats	David O'Dowda	3:42
Le Monde – From Talk To Me	Richard Carter	2:15
Post Human	Lucille Croft	1:31
Diving Woman	Japanese Breakfast	6:33
Into Black	Blouse	3:28
Joyride	Tony Seltzer, Eartheater	2:46
Swimming with the Crocodiles	The Veils	4:32
Outro	M83	4:07
Thin Air (WaterBABii_Miix)	Waterbaby, BABii	4:02
Come Around	070 Shake	1:36
Pyre	Son Lux	4:56
Mute Poetry	El Jazzy Chavo	2:51
Time	Triathlon	4:26
Caught In Time, So Far Away	You'll Never Get to Heaven	3:49
Show Me How	Beacon	2:39
Otherside	Perfume Genius	2:40
Beyond Love	Beach House	4:25
Depth Of My Soul	Thievery Corporation, Shana Halligan	3:23
Red Lights	SAULT	3:04
Possibility	Lykke Li	5:06

1h 51m

(Hedgehog's Dilemma) [Day]

I become a chorus of sighs.

Apartment Song	Really From	4:26
Crush	Cigarettes After Sex	4:26
I Know You Love Me, But Do You Think of Me, Romantically	Charles	2:55
Begin again	Purity Ring	3:37
Hyuwee	Session Victim	3:47
Group Autogenics I	The Books	3:43
Promise You'll Haunt Me	Auscultation	6:33
Ever (Foreign Flag)	Team Sleep	2:51
Walking In Straight Lines	Insides	5:09
vs Reality	AYA GLOOMY	3:24
Shadowww	Loukeman	4:19
Fear of Flying	Bowery Electric	5:39
Sacred Manifestation	Grimez	2:57
Swimming	Breathe Owl Breathe	4:08
CALL ME IN YOUR SUMMER	SHE IS SUMMER	4:23
Everyone Is So In Love With You	Women	3:28
Her Hippo	Dry Cleaning	4:38
Wallflower	Jinjer	4:17
This Is My Beloved	Mort Garson	3:04
A Face Without Eyes	Nmesh	5:59
Casualty	Pional	5:07
When the Sun Hits	Slowdive	4:45
Blue Sky And Yellow Sunflower	Susumu Yokota	3:59
WHIRLPOOL	Kinoko Teikoku	4:28
Holocene	Zella Day, Weyes Blood	4:26
A Time for Us	Joe Pass	3:15
Daysleeper	Dirty Art Club	3:45
Kinky Love	Pale Saints	4:04
Our Dust	A.C. Marias	3:29
The Leanover	Life Without Buildings	5:23
Sunlight Feels Like Bee Stings	HTRK	4:09

2h 10m

(Hedgehog's Dilemma) [Twilight]

I rub my lips across her shoulder blades.

Wildflower	Beach House	3:39
I Want Your Sex	Raissa	3:02
Show Me Your Mind	Sunken	3:33
In Love with It All	Khushi	4:04
Spells	Jenny Hval	6:10
1979	The Smashing Pumpkins	4:26
Infinite Love	Emile Mosseri	2:25
Nina Cried Power	Hozier, Mavis Staples	3:45
I'm with You	GROUPLOVE	5:34
Love Virus	Rollercoaster	4:31
Atlas: Body	Sleeping At Last	3:55
Liquid Smooth	Mitski	2:49
Carly and Caroleカーリーとキャロル	Sekitō Shigeo	3:37
Slow Like Honey	Fiona Apple	5:56
Heaven or Las Vegas	Cocteau Twins	4:58
Whoa	Snoh Aalegra	3:19
Drain You	Nirvana	3:43
When U Saw Love	ELIO, Babygirl	3:26
It Feels Like Floating	Mary Lattimore	11:31
Baby	Helena Deland	4:29
Girl Like Me	Dove Cameron	2:29
Burning Off My Clothes	Sworn Virgins	6:49
Follow It Up	Patrick Holland	3:40
Venus in Leo	HTRK	5:46
Lover // Over the Moon	Alice Phoebe Lou	3:27
You Go To My Head	Billie Holiday	2:54
Cosmic Love	**Florence + The Machine**	**4:15**
Lovers Rock	TV Girl	3:33
Just like Heaven	The Cure	3:32
Kiss City	Blondshell	2:23
Conservation of Two	Sweet Trip	2:39

2h 10m

(Hedgehog's Dilemma) [Night]

I fold my legs into the recess of her legs.

Pink and Gold and Blue	You'll Never Get to Heaven	2:55
Moonlight Rendezvous	The Other People Place	7:07
The Night Has a Thousand Eyes	John Coltrane	6:51
Hedgehog's Dilemma	Shirō Sagisu	2:47
Scenery	Ryo Fukui	5:31
UNDRESS	Passing Currents	4:53
Midnight, The Stars and You	Deerhoof	3:44
Dance PM	Hiroshi Yoshimura	6:32
George's Dilemma	Clifford Brown, Max Roach Quintet	5:36
Two Roomed Motel	Scott Gilmore	4:12
~~	Hidden Spheres	6:32
Tapestry from an Asteroid	Sun Ra	2:07
Nightswimming	R.E.M.	4:18
Pacer	Jesper Ryom	7:39
Some Sort of Paradise	Robin Guthrie	4:04
It's Better with You	Isabel's Dream	4:48
Ginkgo	I Am Robot And Proud	3:39
THOUSAND KNIVES	Ryuichi Sakamoto, Kazumi Watanabe	9:39
Swim and Sleep (Like a Shark)	Unknown Mortal Orchestra	2:45
The Universe In Her Eyes	KiNK	4:14
Music to Soothe the Savage Snake Plant	Mort Garson	3:23
Farther and Fainter	John Tejada	6:19
John Coltrane Interview – (by Carl-Erik Lindgren)	John Coltrane	6:13
Glad To Be Unhappy	Nels Cline	4:07
Your Home	Kuniyuki Takahashi	5:11
Some Jazz Shit	FaltyDL	6:12
Night Lights	**Gerry Mulligan**	**4:52**
Love Is A Dangerous Necessity – Incomplete	Charles Mingus	4:34
Along the Causeway	Fuubutsushi	3:08
Showreel, Pt. 2	DjRUM	9:01
Blink	Hiroshi Yoshimura	4:42

2h 37m

(Heartbreaker) [My Soul Responding]

I watch her leave the way I watch my blood being drawn.

Alia's Intro	Alia Kadir	1:55
Habits of My Heart	Jaymes Young	3:30
Writer In The Dark	Lorde	3:36
Blue Velvet	070 Shake	4:36
Lies in the Eyes of Love	Part Time	3:16
It's You	BØRNS	3:58
I miss u (with Au/Ra)	Jax Jones, Au/Ra	2:52
Habits (Stay High)	Tove Lo, The Chainsmokers	4:24
Serial Heartbreaker	FLETCHER	2:13
Her	Raury	4:16
Alone	Miette Hope	3:38
Icarus	Fana Hues	2:30
Romantic	Mannequin Pussy	2:39
Circles	Post Malone	3:35
Elegy for Love	Kit Sebastian	3:37
I Float Alone	Julee Cruise	4:35
Trophy	TAELA	2:40
Not Because I Loved You	Max Drazen	2:59
Magnified	Island Police	3:57
Arcade	Duncan Laurence, FLETCHER	3:07
Name of Love	Ice Spice	1:46
Fire of Love	Jesse Jo Stark	4:40
Endlessly	Omar Apollo	2:34
Below The Clavicle	Eartheater	3:58
Big Bang	Cherry Glazerr	2:49
Blood Moon	POLIÇA	4:07
Just My Soul Responding	Amber Run	3:58
LOVE BOMB	Kay Marie, RDGLDGRN	2:32
We Had A Good Time	Bullion	3:10
Purple	RETRIEVER	4:21
I Miss You	Alexis Munroe	2:37

1h 44m

(Adonis' Cock) [Mood]

"Everybody wants to love you" — Japanese Breakfast

Let Me In	El Perro del Mar	3:02
Sex on Fire	Kings of Leon	3:23
MIDDLE OF THE NIGHT	Elley Duhé	3:04
It Takes Time To Be A Man	The Rapture	5:42
Everybody Wants to Love You	Japanese Breakfast	2:12
Bend Your Mind	Elysian Fields	3:27
Lust	Boy Harsher	3:05
Good Love	Hannah Laing, RoRo	2:50
I'm Good	Dizzy Fae	2:28
Ride Or Die	Sevdaliza, Villano Antillano	3:05
Chrysalis	Pram	3:57
Penalties of Love	Sequoyah Murray	4:07
mOth	Dua Saleh	2:49
It's Your Thing	The Isley Brothers	2:49
Show My Love for You	Demise	1:54
You Were Right	RÜFÜS DU SOL	3:59
Da Ya Think I'm Sexy?	Revolting Cocks	5:37
Chaos	Louisahhh	3:48
Placeholder for the Night	R. Missing	3:28
Your Name	Bernache	3:07
Bang Bang	GRAE	2:49
Same Damn Time	Future	4:33
It's Not The Worst – Lali Puna Remix	Two Lone Swordsmen, Lali Puna	4:21
Supernatural	BØRNS	3:45
Love's Dart	Django Django	3:50
Pumping	Patti Smith	3:22
Velvet Mood	Alice Phoebe Lou	2:03
Lovin' You, Baby	Charles Bradley, Menahan Street Band	5:28
Masseduction	St. Vincent	3:17
The Future	Leonard Cohen	6:42
Become the Beast	Karliene	4:54

1h 52m

silhouette
swimming

(Hedgehog's Dilemma)

DÉJÀ
VU

DÉJÀ VU

Your Love (Déjà Vu) | Glass Animals

(Essence) Of GOEW

GOEW is freedom.

What is freedom then?

Freedom is the ability to open all doors and pass through them at the same instant.

This kind of freedom is not given to us.

No. So, I wrote GOEW.

The wind! The southwest wind...

Title Cards	ORLANDO	vs	GOEW
1	DEATH		DIVORCE
2	LOVE		SEX
3	POETRY		POETRY
4	POLITICS		DESPAIR
5	SOCIETY		DELIRIUM
6	SEX		ATOPOS
7	BIRTH		BARDO

I undress my hunger as a desire to start over (DTSO).

Inside the coffin was a corpse, but it was not my mother.
It was a mannequin.

I look at the ocean and see all the waves—
I don't follow one wave, far off, to the shore.

It's already happening in each of us (outside language).

AN OPERA

Down On Me | **Sudan Archives**

ADONIS: Do you remember the first time we fucked?
You ordered *The Kitchen Sink*.

We watched *Kids' Baking Championship*.
I went down on you.

You kept saying, *Eat my little pussy*.
Eat that pussy.

It made me manic.
Possessed.

We fucked.
We fell asleep.

I woke up to you touching me.
We fucked again.

Or no.
You made me come with your hands.

We took a shower together.
I drove you home.

You told me you were adopted.
I told you my mom just died.

A GESTALT

If You Stayed Over | Bonobo, Fink

SELENE: I'm unlovable!

ADONIS: No! You're too lovable. I'm unlovable.

SELENE: No! You're too nice. Everybody loves you.

ADONIS: No! They love a singular part of me. They love my generosity. They love my playlists, the car rides home after a night of drinking. Nobody even knows me fully. Except you! You know all of me, and you have fallen out of love with me. I'm a monster!

SELENE: No! You're not a monster. And I haven't fallen out of love with you. It's just... I don't know me! Not all of me. Not yet. I don't have as many parts as you do. So, I feel intimidated. I get shy.

ADONIS: You can hide in me. You are one of my parts. My heart!

SELENE: I don't want to hide in you! I want to bloom. (Sigh) You can help me though. (Smiling) You can suck me. Breathe into my belly all your poetry. Fuck me. Cum inside me. Spend the night. Just hold me. We don't have to talk. Just don't go.

A FLIGHT TO

I Want To Break Free | Queen

ADONIS: Would you move to Paris?

SELENE: Ye.

ADONIS: What about Los Angeles?

SELENE: Ye.

ADONIS: Lima?

SELENE: Ye.

ADONIS: We should just run away!

SELENE: Hm.

ADONIS: I don't want to end up like Gatsby. Or Daisy.

A RECKONING

Ego Death | Ty Dolla $ign, FKA twigs, Skrillex, Kanye West

SELENE: Who is Thaïs?

ADONIS: Ghost.

SELENE: Who is Nico?

ADONIS: Ghost.

SELENE: Who am I then?

ADONIS: Moon. (Sigh) Who is Thaddeus?

SELENE: Gay.

ADONIS: Who is Phil?

SELENE: Gay.

ADONIS: Who am I then?

SELENE: Rent. (Withdrawing)

ADONIS: Did you mean any of the things you said?

SELENE: Some of them. (Sigh) You?

ADONIS: Most of them.

Toast To Posthumous Playlists

I'm the Echo | DARKSIDE

Elegy for Adonis	*"Feu Adonis"*
Myth of Adonis	*"Become your own myth"*
Adonis in Real Life	*"This is no movie"*
MRI Brain w/o Contrast	*"Look closer"*

I felt myself always condemned to go through the wrong door.

No, I felt myself condemned to want to go through the other door
(invariably after going through any door).

To be in constant flight (a bird).
To be in constant freefall (a human).
To be diving, in constant pursuit (a cormorant).

So, GOEW...
To pass through all the doors at once.

Desire is the center of the circle.
Ominous for our swimmer.

What I glimpsed? A silhouette.
And I was aroused.

What we call arousal, dormant
in each of us—waiting, begging, clawing
to be born—to be let out—to inhabit...

To be freed!

Life flows from the bedroom to the street.
This defies decorum.

The point of mortality is to feel pain, and then
to yearn to be pain-free (which is to not exist).

Each person longs to be fiction.

Adonis' tombstone:

RIP

[This] (Life)
"Because I was flesh"
Daddy

SWIMMING

Swim Until You Can't See Land | **Frightened Rabbit**

(Purgatory, RI)

THAÏS: Your book...

GOD: It lacks faith.

ADONIS: I disagree.

THAÏS: Why give it to me?

ADONIS: You're the star!

GOD: You killed her off!

THAÏS: What about Nico? Selene?

ADONIS: They're stars, too.

GOD: Whores!

THAÏS: You know I'm a jealous bitch, right?

ADONIS: Yes.

GOD: Fool.

THAÏS: When I first read it, I was furious! You killed 'us,' I said to myself.

ADONIS: No! Don't say that.

THAÏS: Then I reread it, and I realized what we had, it already died. Your book is its coffin.

ADONIS: Stop! Please.

THAÏS: I'm not upset anymore.

ADONIS: I'm stuck in the book. The way one is stuck in mud...

THAÏS: My Borges.

ADONIS: My Thaïs.

THAÏS: Your love is far away. You are far away. Always wandering off in your head. (Knocking on his temple) Where are you? Who's there with you?

ADONIS: A hotel. A lover.

THAÏS: Which? Who?

ADONIS: All of them. At some point, all of them become 'a lover.'

THAÏS: Why do you haunt me?

ADONIS: Because you love the same way I do.

THAÏS: I love you, the man.

ADONIS: You love me, the poet.

THAÏS: I took pride in being your muse. You took that away from me!

ADONIS: All the poems I wrote for you, they don't go away. They're still yours.

THAÏS: You're out of reach. Still handsome, but out of reach. A real torture! I'm old now, my body is going through changes... Are you still attracted to me?

ADONIS: (Slowly) Yes.

GOD: Liar!

THAÏS: I want to suck you.

ADONIS: No.

THAÏS: Give me your cock.

ADONIS: No, I won't.

THAÏS: You will.

ADONIS: I won't waste your hurt. Or mine.

(Enter Nico)

THAÏS: (Yielding) Another star?

ADONIS: Hello Nico.

NICO: Hello Adonis, my swimmer.

ADONIS: No more hotels?

NICO: Just restaurants now. (To Thais) Hello Thaïs.

THAÏS: (To Nico) You made me into a monster.

GOD: (Imploring) Thaïs!

NICO: Pardon me. Is this a picnic? Is there wine?

ADONIS: Every lover becomes a wife.

GOD: That's when you move on.

ADONIS: That's my curse.

THAÏS: Every wife becomes an x. Like days x-ed out on a calendar.

NICO: A lifetime of x-ed out days, like this guy (nodding at God).

(God shrugs.)

ADONIS: I'd rather that than live the same day over and over again.

THAÏS: (To Nico) Why are you here?

NICO: An accident.

THAÏS: What about Selene? Is she coming too?

GOD: No. She's still alive.

ADONIS: Thank goodness!

GOD: You're welcome.

NICO: (To God) That's not you! Don't take credit.

GOD: The world runs itself.

ADONIS: I'm going for a swim.

NICO: Adieu.

(Adonis walks to the shoreline, undresses, wades into the water. They watch him. He swims out towards the horizon. God scoots closer to Thaïs, puts his arm around her.)

GOD: (To Thaïs) You were always my favorite.

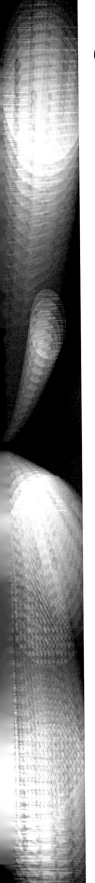

(Theory) Of Adonis

Theory: As Ego goes down, Poetry/Love go up

Intervening variables: Empathy, Judgment, Open-mindedness, Taboos

Moderator variable: Curiosity

How it works (also, see logic model in GOEW):

> As Ego goes down,
> Empathy goes up.
>
> As Empathy goes up,
> Judgment (Dogma) goes down.
>
> As Judgment (Dogma) goes down,
> Open-mindedness goes up.
>
> As Open-mindedness goes up,
> Perception of Taboos goes down.
>
> (The more curious
> The more dramatic the decrease.)
>
> As Perception of Taboos goes down,
> Poetry/Love(-making) go up.
>
> As Poetry/Love(-making) go up...

An Adonis is born.

The inverse is true, too:

As Ego goes up,
Empathy goes down.

As Empathy goes down,
Judgment (Dogma) goes up.

As Judgment (Dogma) goes up,
Open-mindedness goes down.

As Open-mindedness goes down,
Perception of Taboos goes up.

(The more incurious
The more dramatic the increase.)

As Perception of Taboos goes up,
Poetry/Love(-making) go down.

As Poetry/Love(-making) go down...

Brutes are born. (And you? Are you a brute?)

THEY WHO ARE MAKING THE FILM (PRE-PRODUCTION)

Stay Tuned | Robert Wyatt

DEVIL: What kind of hair do you want?

ADONIS: Long hair.

DEVIL: What kind of face?

ADONIS: A handsome one.

DEVIL: Tony Starks' face?

ADONIS: Sure.

DEVIL: What suit do you want?

ADONIS: A track suit.

DEVIL: Do you want headphones?

ADONIS: Yes.

DEVIL: (Stroking his chin) Do you want a girl?

ADONIS: (Aroused) Yes.

DEVIL: What kind of hair, for the girl?

ADONIS: Purple hair.

DEVIL: What kind of body?

ADONIS: Sexy body.

DEVIL: Do you want a bed?

ADONIS: Yes.

DEVIL: What size?

ADONIS: King size.

GOD: (To Devil) Stop encouraging him!

My Cheetah/My Heart

CHEETA1b ms800 | Aphex Twin

(Adonis enters the cheetah's cage)

She's sick
She's depressed
She hates herself

I approach
Aroused, curious
To pet her

She yawns
Her indifference is not grace
It's cunning

I want only one thing
The sublime
To graze her moon-skin

She purrs
'Money'
'Sadness'

I'm sick, too
A mysterious illness
I mind-wander

Lost in 'Memory'
'Music'
'Metaphors'

'Movies' too
But in real life
No one wants help

No one believes
In happiness
No one survives themselves

So, tell me
My cheetah
My heart

Why do I see so well?
Why do I care so much?
She perks up

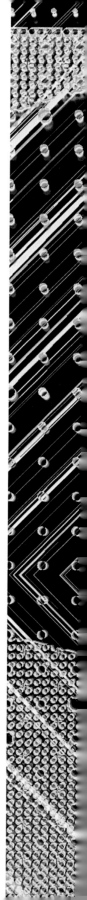

ALTERNATE WORLD, ALTERNATE ENDING

`Easy (Switch Screens)` `Son Lux, Lorde`

SELENE: Friends?

ADONIS: Friends.

SELENE: I need a friend right now.

ADONIS: I know.

SELENE: I won't talk about the past, though.

ADONIS: Ok, just know, when you're confronted with one of your lies, and you hunker down in the lie, and the person who confronted you knows you're lying, you're not saving face by hunkering down. Quite the opposite, actually! And they run from you!

SELENE: That's fair. I acknowledge that.

ADONIS: Thank you.

SELENE: You're welcome. (Eye-gazing) Maybe in the future we can be something.

ADONIS: My spirit's not at peace with you. As a lover.

SELENE: I'd be a good girl for you—if you leave your wife. I'd need you all to myself.

ADONIS: You'd have to be a bad girl all the time, not good. That means taking it in the ass, and telling me when you fuck other guys.

SELENE: Hmph!

ADONIS: Both are hard stops for you, I know.

SELENE: I'd let you fuck my ass. (Adonis rolls his eyes) But it hurts!

ADONIS: If you were good all the time, I wouldn't believe you.

(They smirk at each other. A comfortable silence. Then, Selene rises from the couch.)

SELENE: Come to bed with me.

ADONIS: I'm going to stay on the couch.

SELENE: No! I want you to hold me.

ADONIS: (Hesitantly) Ok, if you change the sheets.

SELENE: (Giddy) Ok.

(They change the sheets. They undress fully. They get into bed together.)

ADONIS: I missed you.

SELENE: I missed you more.

(She crawls under the sheets and sucks him. He doesn't resist. He focuses all his attention on his breathing: inhaling through the nose, expanding the diaphragm, exhaling through the nose. He finds a perfect rhythm. He tickles his nipples with his forefingers. She takes him deeper in her mouth than ever before. He doesn't warn her when he's about to cum. She swallows his cum and keeps sucking. He pulls her up to him. They kiss.)

(On the floor, inside Adonis' pants' pocket is the following note: 'Back into the cheetah cage: 1. Don't believe her (don't expose her lies) 2. Don't sleep with her (tell her, maybe in the future) 3. Be nice (accept her niceness, don't interpret it as wanting you back) 4. Don't pout (don't be heavy) 5. Don't ask (don't tell).' Meanwhile, inside Selene's journal, hidden in her underwear drawer, is the following recent entry: 'Put a new spell on him. Make him your guarantor. Don't let him leave until he agrees.')

My Gemini/My Fiancé

Moment | Victoria Monét

Your breasts out
       The sun
       The moon

Your ass out
       The sunset
       The sunrise

Your pussy out
       Polaris

Your big eyes
       Aurora Borealis

Your big hair
       Umbrella to cosmos

When you undress
For me
And I'm still dressed
       Revelation
       Of universe
       To a mortal

Then you undress me
My cock out
       A mighty oak

You sit on my face
My cock out
       An evergreen

Smell of your ass
In my nostrils
      My breath

Your ass
Slides down/in
      My moment

Your wetness
My cock out/in
      A hydraulic

Bouncing
Up/down
      The tide in/out

Our bodies
      Breaking waves
          Spilling
          Plunging
          Collapsing
          Surging

I fill you
With my essence
      My love (Crystalline)

I don't know
This is last time
We will fuck
      But I know
      Only in sex
      Do I trust you

A RECKONING (REPRISE)

I Know | **Post Malone**

(Rowdy bar)

ADONIS: As a writer, you have to consider the time and audience you are writing to.

GOD: You have to read the room, I always say.

ADONIS: But you also have to consider future or foreign audiences.

GOD: They may be more forgiving, more understanding.

(They clink bottles.)

ADONIS: I'm a fool. I loved someone who didn't love me.

GOD: Selene?

ADONIS: Selene. I helped someone who didn't want my help.

GOD: You were a fool. Now, you know!

ADONIS: What have I done? My poor wife...

GOD: She was just here.

ADONIS: (Startled) What'd she say?

GOD: The same thing you said. But she was talking about you.

ADONIS: (Dismayed) What'd you say?

GOD: The same thing I told you.

ADONIS: Is she leaving me?

GOD: Are you leaving Selene?

ADONIS: Hell yes! (Processing) God, I fucked up!

GOD: (Laughing) You are, my poet-friend, what I call a karma battery.

ADONIS: Huh?

GOD: On one end, you're giving the horns, on the other end, at the same time, you're getting the horns. It's instant poetic justice!

COMPLETE

PLAYLIST
OF

(You Are Here)

CRYSTALLINE

GREEN

Complete Playlist of Crystalline Green (Including Interludes) [Title Cards Version]

"A couple is one who loves plus one who lets love." — Kathy Acker, *Blood and Guts in High School*

Crystalline Green	Goldfrapp	4:28
God's Chariots	Oklou	3:03
Pagan Poetry	Björk	5:14
Screaming Infidelities	Dashboard Confessional	3:33
Don't Sweat The Technique	Eric B. & Rakim	4:22
Alien Observer	Grouper	3:56
The Mysterious Vanishing of Electra	Anna von Hausswolff	6:08
Standing In the Way of Control	Gossip	4:16
I Want You to Want Me - Live at Nippon	Cheap Trick	3:45
Temporarily Yours	Cristina	5:35
Reverie - Above & Beyond Club Mix	Above & Beyond, Zoë Johnston	3:52
Black Out Days	Phantogram	3:47
Paradise	Griff	3:02
No Kink in the Wire	Cosha	5:30
Kill Me With Your Love	One True God	2:54
In a Manner of Speaking	Nouvelle Vague, Camille	3:58
Come on Doom, Let's Party	Emily Wells	3:36
In The Evening (It's So Hard To Tell Who's Going To Love You The Best)	Karen Dalton	4:33
Moonlight Densetsu (From "Sailor Moon")	Harpsona	2:19
Sex Sounds	Lil Tjay	2:42
Fever dream	mxmtoon	3:16
She's A Rainbow	The Rolling Stones	4:11
Bizarre Love Triangle	New Order	4:21
Exist for Love	AURORA	4:12
Moanin'	Charles Mingus	8:02
Heavenly	Cigarettes After Sex	4:48
Daddy	Ramsey	4:26
Caramel	Connan Mockasin	1:55
I Took A Ride	Caroline Rose	5:11
Infinity	Jaymes Young	3:57
From You Animal Machine	Eleni Sikelianos, Roger Green	2:39

New York City	Lenny Kravitz	6:22
LAY U DOWN/SEXY	Baro Sura	3:45
Rewind	Kelela	3:58
Paris (Aeroplane Remix)	Friendly Fires, Aeroplane	7:45
MOONLIGHT	TWICE	3:39
Summertime	My Chemical Romance	4:06
Pearly Gates	Grimez	3:29
Tokyo Drift (Fast & Furious)	Teriyaki Boyz	4:15
No Limit	G-Eazy, A$AP Rocky, Cardi B	4:05
La fête noire	Flavien Berger	6:04
Estranged	Guns N' Roses	9:23
Unearth Me	Oklou	3:25
G.U.Y.	Lady Gaga	3:52
My Body Left My Soul	USERx, Matt Maeson, et al	4:20
Won't	Tanerélle	4:03
Daddy	SAKIMA, ylxr	2:32
Daddy AF	Slayyyter	2:31
Faith Consuming Hope	Eartheater	4:50
SLOW JAMS IN THE DARK	Xoxocouron	2:51
Hallelujah - Live in London	Leonard Cohen	7:20
Rack City	Tyga	3:23
Los Angeles	The Midnight	6:29
Moon Awaits	Beazzo	3:12
Can't Get Enough	Kat Leon, NOCTURN	4:16
Sunflower-Spider-Man: Into the Spider-Verse	Post Malone, Swae Lee	2:38
See You Bleed	Ramsey	3:34
La Flor de Canela	Chabuca Granda	3:20
Cinematic Love	DSRT, BELLSAINT	3:40
L'importante è finire	Mina	3:19
Don't Despair	Lafawndah	5:32
Altered Reality	DreamWeaver, botanical anomaly	3:25
LB	Mar de Copas	4:40
If I Could Find You (Eternity)	The Holydrug Couple	3:00
Night Time, My Time	Sky Ferreira	3:51
The Stage	Shura	4:37
Start Over Again	Cookiee Kawaii	3:30
Cupid De Locke	The Smashing Pumpkins	2:50

Behind the Scenes	Zero, Jess Spink	4:43
Bullets	Smash Into Pieces	3:25
SAD GIRLZ LUV MONEY Remix	Amaarae, Kali Uchis, Moliy	3:25
For Sure	Future Islands	3:25
Foreshadow	ENHYPEN	2:27
Infinity	Infinity Ink	5:08
Lie to Me	Depeche Mode	5:03
Alternate World, Alternate Age	Son Lux	4:20
Fuck Him All Night	Azealia Banks	2:56
100 Miles An Hour	Labrinth	3:01
This Is A Life	Son Lux, Mitski, David Byrne	2:41
Eudaemonia	Them Are Us Too	4:21
Die 4 You	Perfume Genius	3:33
Promise (Reprise)	Akira Yamaoka	1:45
Tadow	Masego, FKJ	5:01
I want to sleep for 1000 years	EKKSTACY	2:15
Spring Is Coming With a Strawberry in the Mouth	Roger Doyle	4:23
Kaleidoscope	Flower Face	3:08
Underwaterfall	Bearcubs	4:20
Reprise (From "Spirited Away") [Piano Version]	Nikolai Tal	1:39
Coming Down	Dum Dum Girls	6:29
Taking My Own Advice	Baird	3:13
EMOTIONAL MASOCHIST	Kent Osborne	2:09
4U	Ojerime	2:16
DEATH FANTASY	Kilo Kish, Miguel	2:09
Shape of Things to Come	Paul Keogh	3:01
False Moon	Them Are Us Too	5:52
Kaleidoscope	Champagne Drip, Crystalline	3:31
Take Me to the Sun	ELSZ	5:14
Overture	Momoko Kikuchi	2:23
Dream Baby Dream	Suicide	6:24
Heart Stop	Wax Tailor, Jennifer Charles	2:55
Otherside	Perfume Genius	2:40
Daysleeper	Dirty Art Club	3:45
Cosmic Love	Florence + The Machine	4:15
Night Lights	Gerry Mulligan	4:52

Just My Soul Responding	Amber Run	3:58
Velvet Mood	Alice Phoebe Lou	2:03
Night Swim	Josef Salvat	5:04
Your Love (Déjà Vu)	Glass Animals	3:54
Séance of Light	Jape	3:57
Down On Me	Sudan Archives	4:10
If You Stayed Over	Bonobo, Fink	5:23
I Want To Break Free	Queen	3:18
Ego Death	Ty Dolla $ign, FKA twigs, et al	3:51
I'm the Echo	DARKSIDE	5:08
Swim Until You Can't See Land	Frightened Rabbit	4:19
Lovedbyyou	LA Vampires, Cologne	4:00
Stay Tuned	Robert Wyatt	3:50
CHEETA1b ms800	Aphex Twin	0:27
Easy (Switch Screens)	Son Lux, Lorde	4:23
Moment	Victoria Monét	2:58
I Know	Post Malone	2:20
Present Tense	Radiohead	5:07
Sunrise	Yeasayer	4:07
Crystalline (Omar Souleyman Remix)	Björk	6:39
Wilmot	The Sabres Of Paradise	8:03
The Mirror Conspiracy	Thievery Corporation	3:45
Lorca	Tim Buckley	9:59
Coded Language	Saul Williams	8:49
The Earth Dies Screaming – 12" Version	UB40	8:21
Monk's Mood	Thelonious Monk, John Coltrane	7:51
DISCLAIMER	Talia Stewart	2:02
Formula	Labrinth	1:31
Real Love	Mary J. Blige	4:30
THE DEATH OF PEACE OF MIND	Bad Omens	4:01
Life Goes On	The Damned	4:03

135 songs, 9h 20min

THE
IN
FEC
TED

(Epilogue)

NUCLEUS

(Dissolution) Of Copyright

The Mirror Conspiracy | Thievery Corporation

I contemplate what'll happen after I'm dead.
How will my lovers learn of my death?
Will all my secrets be revealed?
Will my children understand?

Granted, these are more questions than happenings,
but I do have a peculiar fantasy in which a reader
acquires a list of all the books I read
in the order I read them,

(a library loan sheet with dates would suffice)
and rereads them in similar order,
and in doing so, becomes immortal.
Then, they come find me, and resuscitate me.

No corpse can play a narrator until they can inhabit a mirror.
A mirror means stepping into performance. Or, Exegesis.

Loquela of the Father

Lorca | Tim Buckley

I organize a casting call.
I rent a loft in which to conduct the interviews.
I am one of the actors too.

    (I am devoured by my act.)

They do not know what they audition for.
They are in the dark.
They are the story's actors and its audience.

    (Actors and audience coalesce.)

There is in fact only one role.
A man feigns his suicide,
then lives underground for x years.

    (This mute figure is an angel.)

Then he returns home.
If a home still exists for him, I am fascinated.
If no home exists, the story ends.

    (This text disappears.)

The Moon

Coded Language | Saul Williams

I could see from my window
the moon was coded.

I drew its face on a wall.
It was a face of stone.

I rubbed a rock against my lips.
Did you draw a man or a woman?

I did not answer. I danced alone,
rehearsing the final scene.

This is not a suicide.
This is my good eye.

I could see wind and its likeness.
I could see the moon,

a moon of dust mites crumbling in night,
but you call them *stars*, and you wish on them.

Gravidity

The challenge is to say I love you
without using the words *I*, *Love*, *You*.

Words *Mushroom*, *Cloud* are off-limits too.
In this relationship, there is no certificate of

Marriage, *Naturalization*, *Citizenship*.
A permanent resident is a character in *Dante's Inferno*,

one circle above professional masturbator.
Between the orgasm and the burn, the bladder swells.

When dying, people piss themselves—an erotic gesture.
In this world, there's a tendency to downplay trauma,

exposure to radiation, the words
Earthquake, *Tsunami*, *Trimester*.

Congratulations on your destruction!
Containment surrenders to non-containment.

The Cell

Monk's Mood | Thelonious Monk, John Coltrane

Here (I stick my hand out the window) wind.
Here (I put my hands on my head) a cool breeze.

I'm a jazz man.
Give me Monk or Coltrane.

The world is my rival.
I'm deprived of innocence.

Then, is it nothing for you, to be in jail?
It is the curtain in a theater

where actors get their feet caught.
I'm so tired of clapping.

Which confession do you prefer?
Call them back.

You shouldn't have come.
I live in a cell.

Dear Selene (Reprise)

DISCLAIMER | Talia Stewart

As transparent as I've been
You still don't see me

I'm you
The same

Except more functioning
And financially independent

Vs. dependent
But you're so caught up

In seeing yourself
In every context

As a star (a nymphet)
Awarding yourself

An Oscar
For your performance

(Getting what you really want—
Material things)

Whereas I'm a writer (a poet)
Turned sugar daddy

In pursuit of—
No, not happiness—

An actress
For porn/opera

(Getting what I really want—
Your body/voice)

We're in this world
A match made in SM heaven

Will you still run away with me
Now that you see me?

Now that you know
You'll have an audience

Beyond us?

GOEW Interludes' Playlist Worksheet/Formula

Formula | Labrinth

1. GOEW/WEOG –＿＿＿＿＿＿＿＿＿＿＿＿＿
2. Subtitle –＿＿＿＿＿＿＿＿＿＿＿＿＿
3. Copyright –＿＿＿＿＿＿＿＿＿＿＿＿＿
4. Contents –＿＿＿＿＿＿＿＿＿＿＿＿＿
5. Accompanying songs –＿＿＿＿＿＿＿＿＿＿＿
6. Swensen –＿＿＿＿＿＿＿＿＿＿＿＿＿
7. "Feu Adonis" –＿＿＿＿＿＿＿＿＿＿＿＿＿
8. Rhythmic gymnastics –＿＿＿＿＿＿＿＿＿＿＿
9. Adonis removes condoms –＿＿＿＿＿＿＿＿＿
10. Brossard –＿＿＿＿＿＿＿＿＿＿＿＿＿
11. Roach –＿＿＿＿＿＿＿＿＿＿＿＿＿
12. Falling –＿＿＿＿＿＿＿＿＿＿＿＿＿
13. "Become your own myth" –＿＿＿＿＿＿＿＿＿＿
14. Pardlo –＿＿＿＿＿＿＿＿＿＿＿＿＿
15. Wedding cake –＿＿＿＿＿＿＿＿＿＿＿＿＿
16. Portrait of Adonis –＿＿＿＿＿＿＿＿＿＿＿＿
17. Adonis' cock –＿＿＿＿＿＿＿＿＿＿＿＿＿
18. Sharks –＿＿＿＿＿＿＿＿＿＿＿＿＿
19. "This is no movie" –＿＿＿＿＿＿＿＿＿＿＿＿
20. Patchen –＿＿＿＿＿＿＿＿＿＿＿＿＿
21. Pole dancing –＿＿＿＿＿＿＿＿＿＿＿＿＿
22. Fireworks –＿＿＿＿＿＿＿＿＿＿＿＿＿
23. "Look closer" –＿＿＿＿＿＿＿＿＿＿＿＿＿
24. Genet –＿＿＿＿＿＿＿＿＿＿＿＿＿
25. Bullseye –＿＿＿＿＿＿＿＿＿＿＿＿＿
26. Adonis contemplates tiny corpses –＿＿＿＿＿＿＿
27. Adonis lies down –＿＿＿＿＿＿＿＿＿＿＿＿
28. Complete list of characters –＿＿＿＿＿＿＿＿＿
29. Index of poems –＿＿＿＿＿＿＿＿＿＿＿＿
30. Index of images –＿＿＿＿＿＿＿＿＿＿＿＿＿
31 I see you/seeing me –＿＿＿＿＿＿＿＿＿＿＿＿

The title represents the theme, i.e. what is being inhabited.
The subtitle is a metonym for the theme, and an excerpt from track 27. Each playlist has 31 songs.

Track	Corresponding themes song inhabits
1	= many moods, containing multitudes
2	= sexual ("sex" in song title)
3	= authorship, signature, style
4	= GOEW themes, playlist theme
5	= mise-en-scène, airy, ambient
6	= ballad, awakening, agency
7	= memorial, elegy (instrumental)
8	= choreography, dance music
9	= change, new beginning
10	= eavesdropping, private conversation (foreign language)
11	= ugly-beautiful, beautiful-ugly, harsh truth
12	= losing control, submitting, letting go
13	= manifest, growth (instrumental)
14	= transformation, metamorphosis, sublime (80s/90s hit)
15	= marriage, divorce, cunnilingus
16	= handsome, obsession, love
17	= phallic, ego, carnal
18	= danger, excitement, conflict
19	= circumstance, revelatory, reality (instrumental)
20	= double-faced, masked, conflicted
21	= lap dance, trap music, sexual
22	= breath, kink, explosive
23	= disclosure, discovery (instrumental)
24	= altered, backstory, influence
25	= dagger, killshot, x-marks-the-spot
26	= addiction, blood, post-coital
27	= death, ascension, dream (subtitle of playlist)
28	= found/lost love, disco ("love" in song title)
29	= polyglossia, philosophical
30	= performative, politically incorrect ("kiss" in song lyrics)
31	= insight, mirror, mirroring

OPEN MIC' NIGHT
(DEVIL UPSTAGES GOD)

Real Love | **Mary J. Blige**

DEVIL: Unconditional love?
What!
Hell no!
There's no such thing.
Let's be honest...

When a woman asks
If you'll love her unconditionally,
What she's really asking is
If you'll love her
If she gets fat!

Yup!
That woman is worried.
She sees her mother.
She sees her grandmother.
She sees her sister.

But ok,
I get it,
It's fair,
We all get a little bigger.
A little bit fat is ok,

But there's a limit to my understanding.
I like a little extra cushion,
But if she gets too fat,
If I'm going to break my back,
I'm gone!

I'm out the door!
She's not catching me.
She can't run!
It's *The Great Escape,*
Fat Housewives of New York edition...

Now,
When a man asks a woman
If she'll love him unconditionally,
What he's really asking is
If he can fuck other women, too!

Oh yeah!
It's all about setting the terms.
That's real.
That's honest.
There's no such thing as no matter what.

How do you explain divorce?
How do you explain the love/hate continuum?
All love is conditional,
Based on reciprocation and
What have you done for me lately?

Yeah man.
Anyone who says otherwise is lying.
I tell my wife,
You want me to stick around,
Learn how to deepthroat,

I'll stay at least five years,
Learn how to take it in the ass,
I won't go anywhere for a decade,
Learn how to cook,
You got me for life!

She tells me,
You keep eating that pussy,
That's good for five years.
You keep eating that ass
That's good for five more,

You keep lasting until I come first,
That's an easy decade,
You keep paying that mortgage and car lease,
And for my mani-pedis,
You got me for life!

That's real love.
All that other bullshit is fantasy.
You got to work for real love.
Nothing is free.
Nothing lasts forever.

(Later that night at a dive bar.)

GOD: (Drunk) You have to ask yourself, in every relationship, are you the one who is secure in your feelings, or are you the one who is insecure? Are you a homebody, or do you like to go out? Are you content, or are you constantly dreaming, yearning for something more? Are you the one who loves more than you are loved? Or, are you the one who is loved more? Because every relationship breaks down this way, you're one or the other. There are no equals in a relationship. It's a zero-sum game of content vs discontent, happy vs curious, a wandering mind... (incoherent). Because if you're the one that's content, and at home, and happy (snorts), well then, you're the one that's being cheated on! (Gulping)

BARTENDER: (Chuckles) People choose what they want, and what's easiest. You have to trust that. Now, some might choose what they want, if they want it bad enough, even if it's not easy. And some might choose what's easy even if it's not exactly what they want. But none choose what they don't want *and* what's not easy. The moment that happens, they're gone! Or they're changing things up, that's for sure.

Five Deaths

1. & 2. Death by jumping (tower, bridge)
3. Death by gunfire (reading poem)
4. Death by heart attack (having sex)
5. Death by poison (drinking *Last Word*)

Adonis died in 2020. He returned in 2021. He then died three times, with brief revivals in-between, in 2023: winter (January), spring (March), and summer (June). He returned in fall 2023 as a truthsayer only to die permanently in summer 2024. June 20, 2024 is the exact date of final death. It coincided with the summer solstice. He was just shy of 50 years old.

QUINDECIM BAR

Life Goes On | **The Damned**

BARTENDER: Welcome.

SELENE: (Sitting at bar) This place is to die for!

ADONIS: (Standing at bar) I prefer *Do or Dive*.

BARTENDER: (Pouring two drinks) Let's play a game. However, you should know, the outcome of this game will have grave consequences. For the loser, especially.

SELENE: (Sipping) This is so good!

ADONIS: What's the game?

BARTENDER: Truth or dare.

SELENE: I love this game! I always choose truth, and then I lie anyway! (Flirting)

ADONIS: I hate this game. I always believe her. (Sipping)

BARTENDER: Well, this will be different. If you choose truth, you will tell the truth. I have already made sure of that. (Tapping their drinks) And if you choose dare, the dare will involve you risking your life, with only a fifteen percent chance of surviving.

SELENE: (To Adonis) If you wanted honesty, you should've said.

ADONIS: (To Selene) I did! A hundred times!

BARTENDER: (To Selene) We'll start with you. Truth or dare?

SELENE: Truth.

BARTENDER: Did you see him as a viable lover?

SELENE: No. Because he was much older, and married! (Gasping)

BARTENDER: (To Adonis) Truth or dare?

ADONIS: Truth.

BARTENDER: Did you see her as a viable lover?

ADONIS: Yes. Then, no. I turned my world upside down to be with her. Because I thought it was worth it. I thought she really loved me, and I couldn't leave her believing that.

BARTENDER: But in the end, you did leave her.

ADONIS: Only because I realized she didn't love me. She was gaslighting me the whole time.

BARTENDER: I don't understand. How did you go from believing she loved you to realizing she was gaslighting you?

ADONIS: I mean, the signs were there, but I wanted to believe her, you know. It made for a great story. I fell in love with the story.

SELENE: It's a horrible story! I compromised so much.

ADONIS: (Defensive) I didn't ask you to compromise anything. I asked you what you wanted, and then I gave it to you! I thought if I gave you what you wanted, you'd be grateful, and give me what I wanted.

SELENE: To fuck all the time!

ADONIS: Yes. What's wrong with that? We used to fuck all the time and it was amazing.

SELENE: It was fun, and then it wasn't. It became a chore.

ADONIS: (Sulking) Everything I thought was grace was just tolerance. Our whole relationship, you viewed it as a job.

SELENE: Yes. It was a means to an end. Rent, dinners, trips. Someone to be in the room with me. I can't be alone!

ADONIS: I know. (Sitting) But your loneliness isn't physical. It's in here (pointing to her heart). You lie to and deceive everyone. No one knows the real you.

SELENE: You lie and deceive too!

ADONIS: Not to you! I was lying to and deceiving my wife. That's different.

SELENE: No, it's not.

ADONIS: I was faithful for fifteen years before I cheated. And then I still provided for her, and took care of her. I was a giver. You, you're a taker. A leach! You've never been faithful to any of your lovers, not even fifteen days!

SELENE: I'm 24 years old, moron! I don't know what I want! I make mistakes! So what! Fuck you!

ADONIS: I know. I'm sorry. (Sighing) I'm not the person I was at 24. No one is.

SELENE: I have no one in this world. I have to take care of myself. My parents are shit. My friends are shit. I'm completely on my own. I have to do what's best for me. Sorry if you got hurt along the way. But you're a big boy.

ADONIS: You're right. I'm sorry. I made things heavy. It's just, the nights we were together, (Glancing at the bartender) I felt like a thief in heaven. I knew it was too good to be true. I knew the check would come due, eventually.

SELENE: I just need someone to take care of me, and never leave me alone. And to let me do whatever I want, whenever I want. Because I didn't get to have a childhood like yours, or the high school or college experiences you had. I never got to do anything.

BARTENDER: (Joining both palms) Next round. (To Selene) Truth or dare?

SELENE: Dare.

ADONIS: (Grasping) Me too. Dare.

BARTENDER: Ok. (Lining up twenty pre-poured drinks) Seventeen of these drinks are fatally poisoned. I dare each of you to gulp one.

SELENE: Fuck it! (Gulping)

ADONIS: It's still a great story, minus the happy ending. (Gulping)

BARTENDER: Thank you for playing. Chance will now judge your souls. (Bowing)

SELENE: (Shrugging)

ADONIS: (Sullen) I couldn't stay. Whoever stays is who you deceive the most, and desire the least.